Boxes

Boxes

Jeanette Scales

Nine-year-old Max Pietrowski and his pals interrupt a German sabotage strike in a Massachusetts weapons factory during WWII, causing years-long consequences for all involved, and ending in a resolution none of them could have predicted.

Boxes

ISBN: 978-0-9968223-0-5

Book design by **Arc Manor (www.arcmanor.com)**

Published by **Robbins Press, Quincy, Massachusetts.**

Printed in the United States of America

Acknowledgments

Thanks to my sons Michael, Christopher, Brian, Stephen, and Matthew for their insightful suggestions, and to my grandson Evan of Evan Scales Visuals for his creative work on the cover. Thanks to the writers in my critique group, Cindy Davis, Jennifer Carson, Diedre Currier, and Thomas Greenlaw for their their editorial expertise and encouragement. And thanks to my readers, Nancy McLean, Ella Casey, Suzanne Connary, and Susan Coleman for their suggestions and enthusiastic support.

Author's note

Boxes is a work of historical fiction. Some events are as true to life as my research allowed, some are as I considered they might have happened according to the circumstances, and others, as well as the characters, are from my imagination.

CONTENTS

Two fathers separated by the Atlantic Ocean, relocated to create a better life for their families. They did ... until their sons crossed paths.

1

Otto Mueller

Germany, 1933

Despite Berlin's brilliant sunshine on 11 May, my hands were cold. I thrust them into the pockets of my suit jacket, now two sizes too big, and discovered the stub I'd saved of my last cigarette. I lit up and stepped aside as three German soldiers swaggered past, smoking and laughing at a shared joke. The military were everywhere, watching and listening.

I was on my way home after spending another day outside factories with dozens of other men failing to find work. Savoring a drag on my cigarette I approached the park where I'd played as a child. A chill ran up my spine. A high wire fence around the park's perimeter cordoned off a forest of tents for the German Army Troops billeted there. Trucks for equipment and personnel chugged across the fields. Soldiers marched on roads where trees had been.

Only last summer Trudy and I brought our nine-year-old Katrina and her eleven-year-old brother, Heinrich, to picnic on the grassy slopes. The children romped through the purple heather and hid behind the trees. The sun warmed Trudy and me as we sat on a blanket under an old oak, watching our healthy, carefree children play. We never imagined our lives could change in an instant. Two weeks after our picnic, my engineering firm closed its doors.

I reached the stone pillars at the entrance of the park, and froze. The fence spanning the opening was covered with a sign, "Attention! Keep Out! Military Personnel Only. Trespassers Will Be Punished." So this is what my city has become, a fortress. It'll never again be the place I loved as a child.

That's it! We must leave Berlin. Better yet, we'll leave Germany. With Hitler's Nazi Party in charge the entire country will suffer frightening changes. I took the last pull of my cigarette and stomped it out. "Yes. We'll leave Germany."

A tightness gripped my chest as soon as I said the words out loud. Acting on my choice would not be as easy as making it. As if to dissuade me, childhood memories flooded my mind. I remembered dinner parties at our house with guests sharing good food, lively conversation, and robust German music. Berlin had been a cosmopolitan, liberal city then, with a diverse population of interesting people. My father held a Professorship in Philosophy at Berlin University, and Mother made sure our family enjoyed all the cultural activities the city had to offer.

I remembered telling my parents, "I want to design and build bridges that will be used every day by German people." At university I soaked up the coursework, practiced my drawing skills, and became a civil engineer. The most prestigious design firm in Berlin hired me at a generous salary.

I didn't see it coming ... this evil depression. Businesses I'd known all my life closed. Surviving businesses super-inflated their prices. Lately we couldn't even buy a loaf of bread. Only a year before I couldn't have imagined it, but German people were starving to death.

Seems it started years ago in Versailles, with the treaty that ended the Great War. We lost, so we had to pay. Reparations they called it. But President Von Hindenburg rallied. He borrowed huge sums of money from American bankers. Kept us going, until the American banks crashed in '29. No more loans. Our economy collapsed. Last January I think the president tried to restore a semblance of normality with his appointment of the popular Adolph Hitler as Chancellor.

Our friend Dieter Kossel saw the catastrophe coming. He left for America six months ago. His letter last week told us about President Roosevelt's New Deal to put US citizens back to work during their depression. He said two new agencies needed engineers to design schools, roads, bridges. I never thought I'd consider leaving my beloved city, but it was the only thing that made sense.

I squared my shoulders, looked straight ahead, and picked up the pace. Trudy would need convincing. I thought about how I'd tell her, and began to practice my proclamation. I reached home, barged into the apartment, and burst out, "We have to leave Berlin."

"No, Otto, it will be fine. Just be patient." Trudy continued to cut up two potatoes and a carrot to make a soup for dinner. She reached up with the back of her hand to flick a golden curl that had escaped from under her kerchief. "This is our home. The new Chancellor promises to make improvements in the economy."

She is so lovely. Even in that old blue housedress and faded apron, she radiates elegance and grace. In another time ours would be an idyllic family, but here, now, life is unbearable. She is the most important person on earth to me, and I'm about to upset her.

I took a deep breath and stepped forward. "Sweetheart, there's no work for me here, and no food in the pantry. Hitler's regime is making life in Berlin worse every day. He's confiscated the newspapers, so whatever we read in the press is censored. And some of my father's most prestigious colleagues at the university were fired last month because of Hitler's new law that non-Aryans can't work for the state, even as teachers ... at any level."

Catching myself shouting, I lowered my voice so I wouldn't frighten Heinrich and Katrina in the next room. "Last night the Nazis burned German books all night. Hitler wants to erase our heritage, to rule, absolutely, over obedient German citizens. This is not how I want to raise our children. I want to emigrate to America."

Trudy twisted toward me, her wide blue eyes searching my face in disbelief. "No! I can't leave my parents. And what about our things ... our furniture and my china."

Tears filled her eyes. My heart ached seeing the pain I had caused. I took her in my arms, trying to comfort us both. "We'll sell what we can, and the rest we'll just have to leave behind. I'll borrow whatever my parents can spare for the trip and book passage tomorrow. We'll sail on the *Bremen* and be in New York in a week."

The next few days blended into a stream of wrenching decisions for Trudy. "I love my things," she said. "I collected our linens, one piece at a time, since before we were married. And I feel your parents' love whenever I handle the Bavarian china they gave us. It's important to be surrounded by beautiful things, Otto, especially when times are so hard. How can I decide what to leave?"

"Remind yourself that we're doing this for our family's survival. Don't you want our children to be as happy as we were growing up? I know how hard it is for you. Maybe you can choose one or two pieces that will remind you of the best times here, and give the rest to people you know will treasure them. We'll walk away knowing we can start collecting beautiful things again in America."

Several nights that week Trudy got up from bed, went into the parlor, and wept quietly. I questioned my decision, but whenever I wavered, the grim certainty of our situation shook me back to reality. We left Berlin on May 19th.

On board ship I sent a telegram to our former neighbors Dieter and Anna Kossel: "Arriving New York Harbor on SS *Bremen,* Saturday, May 26th, 2:00 pm. Can you meet us? Thank you, Otto and Trudy."

On Saturday Dieter, Anna, and their three girls waited for us at the end of the gangplank with shouts of, "Welcome to America," in both German and English. "We have so much to show you about your new country," Dieter said with a broad grin. "How was the sail?"

"Thankfully uneventful," I replied. The children skipped ahead, and after picking up our sparse luggage, we headed for the car lot. Dieter lowered the tailgate of a boxy black car with wooden sides.

"What's this?" I asked. "Nothing like this in Europe."

"It's called a Woody Station Wagon. Made by Dodge. We needed something big enough for our three kids and all their stuff." Heinrich climbed in with Trudy and me while the four girls jumped into the seats way in the back.

On the road, Dieter shared the plans he and Anna had devised for us. "You'll stay with us in Beechwood, it's a hamlet on Long Island, until you find a place of your own. But the first thing you must do is become American citizens. Then you're entitled to all the freedoms of any native born American, and the children are automatically naturalized citizens when you are. Also, I know the children will learn English in school, but it's a good idea for you two to learn it as well."

Anna turned and grinned at us. "You'll be fluent in no time. We're so happy you're here."

We drove through the center of Beechwood. It reminded me of some of the smaller villages in Germany. Shops, a library, and a bank filled the Main Street, but we could see no museums, art galleries, or spots for nightlife. When I mentioned the differences between Beechwood and Berlin, Anna said, "True, but New York City is less than an hour away with theaters, museums, and universities. Best of all, here in America we're free to speak and to live however we choose. There's a severe depression here, no doubting that, with twenty-five percent unemployment. But, there's an optimism too, and a faith in our new president. We've found the people to be just as friendly and helpful here as at home. And Dieter has found enough work to keep us afloat. It's not Berlin, but we've grown to love America."

After a week we found a three bedroom bungalow for rent two streets away from the Kossels. As soon as we were settled, Trudy and I started making the trek to The New School in New York City to study for our citizenship papers. We had classes in English and US history. Trudy was reluctant. "It feels like I'm abandoning my Germany, like I'm a traitor to my heritage. That oath! How can I say it? I 'renounce allegiance and fidelity' to my Germany? I don't!"

"It's for the sake of our family, Trudy. Dedicate the hard work to the children if it helps. I'll always love the Germany we grew up in too, but that's gone forever, and we're here now. We can make a good life in America if we become citizens."

We passed the tests and took the Naturalization Oath in September, allowing me to apply for work with the federally funded Public Works Administration. Because of my education and experience, the agency hired me right away. That day, on the way home from the PWA office, I splurged on a bottle of wine and a dozen roses for Trudy.

Two weeks later, Dieter invited me to attend a meeting of a group called Friends of a New Germany. As soon as I heard the men chatting in a melt of German and English, I felt a kinship with these Beechwood neighbors. Time flew by as we shared stories of our lives back home before the depression. Even those who'd been in America for a while grabbed a German word when English wouldn't suffice.

"If the purpose of the Friends is to help new German immigrants," I said to Dieter on the way home, "the first thing I'm suggesting is that we have evening courses here in Beechwood for citizenship and English. Traveling into the city is a chore." I volunteered for the Citizenship Committee, and we convinced the school board to launch an ongoing Adult Education Program at Beechwood High School.

Besides the club meetings, social gatherings for the whole family happened at a local café. The menu at *Hofbrauhaus* included German potato pancakes, *schnitzel*, and my favorite food, *currywurst*. The aroma of that sausage transported me back to my old Berlin. Feasts ended with black forest cake, cinnamon spice cookies, and dark beer. A small band, dressed in lederhosen, played the stirring German songs I remembered from my childhood.

During one Saturday afternoon gathering at the café, I watched our children break into laughter as they played a game with their new friends. Trudy chatted with the other German women, and I had meaningful work with wages that covered our needs. *This move to America was the right thing to do. Life is good.*

The Friends of a New Germany reorganized in 1936, becoming one of many German/American Bunds, a club similar to the Friends, but with a twist. The new club application contained a statement that the applicant is of the Aryan Race, is free from Jewish or colored blood, and is willing to swear to abide by the "leadership principle," an oath of allegiance to the group leader. The document so reeked of Nazism that I refused to sign it.

"I've decided," I told Trudy and the children, "that we're not going to be German club members anymore."

Heinrich and Katrina protested, "But Papa, our friends are there. Please, Papa."

Trudy intervened, sending the children to play outside in the yard and asked, "Why?"

"The new rules, Trudy. The Nazis are taking over the club."

For the first time in our marriage, my wife stood up to me, arguing, "Otto, I left Berlin and came to America with you because you're my husband, and I love you. But this is outrageous. The club members are the best friends the children and I have here. It's like a bit of home in America. I won't let you take that away from them, or from me, because of some philosophical disagreement. We can protect the children from the politics, but please, don't erase the best part of our social life here because of a few new rules."

The strength of her objections surprised me. I didn't want to forego the club's benefits for our family either. I decided I'd just have to be diligent to counter any Nazi ideas the children might pick up. Anyway, the Nazis couldn't touch us here in America. I relented.

When I saw the swastika on stage between the American and German flags at the next club meeting, an angry heat spread from my belly to my throat. I rose to walk out, but Dieter stopped me, coaxing me to stay and avoid a scene.

The new club leader, Gus Klein, stood at the podium, paused, and began his speech in a hushed voice, capturing the attention of every man in the room. "I am an American citizen ... and I love America." He leaned on the podium and made eye contact with his audience. "It is, after all, fundamentally a German culture with its disciplined work ethic and sense of loyalty. Millions of German-born citizens live here in America. Imagine our power if we could unite. We could restructure America and make it a stronger nation, more like the new Germany."

Raising his voice and his arms to include the entire room, he said, "Before it's too late, we need to join with other German/Americans to take our rightful place in American government. We would then have the power to refute the Declaration of Independence and to repeal the Constitution and Bill of Rights, those death traps of racial and civil equality that dilute our American culture."

Squinting and pointing a finger to every corner of the room, he challenged the members, "Tell Mr. Roosevelt that we, German/Americans, want to abolish the documents that weaken our nation." Raising both arms in an embrace of the room, he declared, "It is our duty, now, to make the United States a stronger, German America!"

Applause exploded. The members gave Klein a standing ovation. He seemed to hypnotize the mild-mannered members of the club. For the first time in my experience in America, the friends I'd known for three years responded in kind when Klein gave the hand salute "*Seig Heil!*"

Incredible! I couldn't breathe. My face burned. I felt dizzy. I stormed out of the room, needing fresh air.

At the café after the meeting, I stopped Klein as he walked by our table. Standing eye to eye with my hand on his arm, I confronted him. "How can you suggest repealing our founding documents? They give you the liberty to speak against the government without fearing reprisal. You must know that most Germans here are against your ideas. That speech you gave stirs emotions, making men do things they'll regret. Don't be surprised if you're opposed as club leader at the end of your term."

Klein's face reddened. He peered into my eyes. "We can discuss our differences later." He jerked his arm from my grasp and walked away.

When I returned to the table, Dieter grabbed my arm. "Please, Otto, be more careful about expressing yourself so openly."

My throat dry, my head throbbing, I said, "That man wants to be Hitler in America."

"Not so loud, Otto. Someone might hear you."

"You see? We're in America, free to say anything we want, but we're still afraid the Gestapo might be listening." I leaned closer to my friend. "Look, I love my fatherland too, but not the regime that's destroying it. Those devils have power only because the German people allow it. We can't let them get a stronghold here as well. We have to speak the truth and keep America healthy."

"I agree, Otto, but it would be wiser to be more diplomatic. Let's have a beer." We both enjoyed a German beer and calmed down while the band played. Dieter accepted the invitation for a game of Skat, and a ride home. I left the cafe, imagining the moment when my head would hit the pillow. As I walked to my car, two men dressed in suits stepped from the alley beside the café, squeezing between me and the street.

One of the men said, "We'd like to talk to you, Mr. Mueller, about your anti-German philosophy. We think maybe you should take a trip back to Germany, to get re-educated."

The other man chimed in, "You need to learn to appreciate the new Germany. Then maybe you could work with your fellow Bund members toward bringing those ideas to America. You need to honor the pledge you signed to follow your Bund's leader."

This one nudged my shoulder, pushing me back toward the cafe. I could smell the whiskey on his breath. The light from the streetlamp bared the sneer on his face. Then Klein emerged from the shadows deep in the alley. "Otto, I'd like to introduce Herr Braun and Herr Schroder, members of the Gestapo."

"Get out of my way. I'm not going anywhere." I planted my feet to stand my ground while trying to shake off their paws. Determined to make them suffer the consequences of their assault, I spit out a threat. "I'm an American citizen. You have no authority here. Move out of my way or I'll call the police."

Time stood still for a split second. I took a decisive step toward the street and my car, believing in that moment that my warning had worked. Then two meat-hook arms grabbed each side of me and pulled me deeper into the alley. A burst of terror flashed through me. I shouted, "No! Let go of me! Get your hands off me!"

They pinned my upper body, but my legs and feet were free. I thrashed to get away, kicking and writhing to escape. I fought for my life. I screamed. "Let go. Help! Someone help!"

But no one walked on the street, and no one inside the café could hear me over the blaring music. Schroder coiled his right arm and hooked his fist sharply into my diaphragm. I crumbled to the ground, not a wisp of breath in me. Knowing I was a dead man if I didn't get away from them, I willed my legs to move. With a growl from my gut, I lunged in the direction of the car.

The flick of something metal caught the corner of my eye. Braun had pulled a pistol from the pocket of his jacket. He held it by the muzzle, and raised his arm. I strained with everything I had to break Schroder's grasp. The gun came down, wielding a chop to the back of my neck. Pain radiated into my head, and down through my shoulder. I lost my footing. I hit the ground. One of the attackers grabbed my head and slammed it into the alley pavement, once, twice ... blackness.

Gus Klein watched as Schroder bashed Otto's head onto the pavement and Braun kicked his body. Braun aimed the Lugar, but shooting wasn't necessary. Otto lay lifeless.

Schroder stood, panting to catch his breath. "His own fault. He shouldn't have fought. If he'd just cooperated he could still be alive with only a few bruises and a new conviction to do the right thing."

"What'll we do with him?" Klein asked.

"What if he had an accident ... a hit and run." Braun replaced his luger. "What a shame that would be."

The men dragged Otto's body out of the alley and dropped it onto the street. Braun made an anonymous phone call to the police.

2

Heinrich Mueller

Mama endured hectic days of police interviews after the shock and denial of losing Papa. Hit-and-run elevated the incident from a possible accident to the crime of negligent homicide, obliging the detectives to make a thorough investigation. She asked herself, and us, what could have distracted Papa so much that he would dash, "blindly into the street," as the witness said? The call from the witness couldn't be traced, and the driver who hit Papa could never be found.

At Papa's funeral my mother told her friend Anna, "I feel adrift. As though I've lost my anchor."

"Dieter misses his best friend terribly," Anna said, her arm around Mama's shoulder. "He has some crazy notions about what happened, trying to make sense of it I think. He may tell you some day. We'll be here for you, always."

I tried to be the strong one, but sometimes Mama, Katrina, and I hugged and cried together. Papa had been our bedrock, the foundation for our family. When I remembered the caring, brilliant man who had been my papa, a weight crushed my chest and a lump closed my throat, banning any words.

The Bund members were considerate, confirming for Mama that they were her genuine friends. They brought dishes of food, and tried to cheer her up, but the anguished expressions on their faces revealed their concern for us. Mama confided to Katrina and me that she wished we could all be in the comfort of her mother's arms. Phone calls sufficed.

Papa's insurance policy covered the cost of the funeral, but after three weeks the reality of unpaid bills confronted us. "I have to look for work," Mama said. I tried to get a job after school at Miller's Hardware Store or Atlantic Grocery, but no one would hire a fourteen-year-old. I vowed that, as soon as I could, I'd get a job with a salary good enough to support Mama and Trini.

Mama had no experience working outside our home. Her friends in the Bund encouraged her to apply for the job in the club office that Gus Klein had advertised. When he interviewed her, Gus hired Mama on the spot. He arranged her work hours while Katrina and I were in school, which Mama greatly appreciated, and he paid her a generous wage.

Mama's job kept her busy for the next few months. She reported to us at dinner one night that she had scheduled a meeting for the Bund Directors with landowners in nearby Yarmouth. The Bund wanted to negotiate the purchase of land for a German/American summer youth camp. Katrina and I couldn't stop grinning about the idea of going to camp.

The directors purchased eleven wooded acres on a lake, with a two-story chalet style house. Mama filled out and submitted the applications for the appropriate permits from the Zoning Board of Yarmouth. Then she and Gus pulled Camp Klein together. The work kept her mind off Papa.

At the dinner table one night I said, "You're doing a great job at the office, Mama. Things you've never done before. And it's your first job. Trini and I are proud of you."

"Thanks, son. Then help me seal these invitation envelopes. Call Katrina back to the table to help too. There are hundreds of them to be mailed to Bund members around America. We want German/Americans to visit our beautiful site, and enroll their children for camp."

Gus arranged for a Long Island Railroad train to depart Flatbush, Brooklyn, on Sunday mornings to bring visitors to Yarmouth. The deluge of positive responses to our mailing stunned Mama and Gus. By the middle of July, the camp leaders had set up the first tents, and dozens of campers, including me and Katrina, cleared land to make more tent platforms. We cut down small trees and dug up the roots. Boys and girls worked hard together. Katrina and I went to camp free of charge so Mama could continue to do her job. The chalet was our dining space, and visiting parents stayed there overnight.

Mama created colorful, educational flyers for Gus, explaining the cultural and economic benefits of an America based on the values of the new Germany. Campers took boxes of them to be distributed back in their hometowns when they left Camp Klein. They were told to leave fliers in student lockers, on car windshields, or pass them out to citizens on the street. Gus said he wanted to flood America with German ideas.

Mama came home from work wearing a big smile one afternoon. She gathered Trini and I for some exciting news. "C'mere Kids. Listen to this. When I started to book Gus's passage on the *Bremen* to attend the Olympic Games in Berlin, he suggested we all go with him. He said with my knowledge of Berlin I'd be a perfect tour guide, and he needed someone to make appointments for him while he's there ... and, the best part, we can visit Oma and Opa Schneider! It'll be heaven." As soon as Mama thanked Gus and accepted his offer, she wired her parents that we would be "home for a week."

When our grandparents met the ship on July 30th, Mama fell into their arms weeping. Hot tears rolled down my cheeks too. Papa should be here with us.

After introductions Gus left for Berlin's Hotel Adlon, while Mama, Katrina, and I went to stay at our grandparents' home. "You wouldn't believe my job." Mama sat on the sofa next to her mom. "I'm more like an assistant than a secretary. Gus lets me design all the literature for the Bund and the Camp. And you should see the campsite. It's so beautiful. There's a lake, and deep woods, and there are already a hundred campers signed up."

She looked happy for the first time since Papa died.

Oma cared for us kids during the day. She was most cheerful in the kitchen with her apron on, cooking for us. She pampered us with our favorite *spaetzle* noodles, *schnitzel*, and spicy cookies. Our little family healed in the glow of our grandparents' home.

After dinner one night, Opa told Mama, "The German economy has improved with the government's new labor programs. Your mother and I have great faith in Hitler's regime."

"But I noticed that the cobbler shop and the book store are closed. Is that because they're owned by Jewish people?" Mama asked.

Oma folded her arms across her chest. "Oh, we don't know about that. We're not political. We're only little people. Those two families left one after the other in the middle of the night, no warning, no goodbyes."

Our kind and loving grandfather's next words seemed to stun Mama. "Jews are different. Good riddance. More jobs for Germans."

Mama's job included picking up tickets for Gus and his guests to attend the Olympic Opening Ceremonies and some of the events. "I'm surprised I'm having so much trouble arranging a meeting between the Chancellor and Gus," she told us. "After all, he represents German citizens living in America. He is a bit flamboyant, and the Chancellor seems to be keeping a low profile on his activities liberating European countries. But this war in Europe has nothing to do with us. America will never get involved."

Mama's persistence paid off. She secured a moment's audience for Gus to meet with the Chancellor, time enough for her to take a photo of the two men. Gus showed it to the Bund members later as evidence of his friendship with Hitler.

Toward the end of the week I found Katrina gazing out the window in our grandparents' parlor. "Hey, Trini, what's the matter? Lose your best pal?"

"I miss my friends, and my dance class. I love visiting with Oma and Opa, but even after we leave on Saturday it'll still be a week to get back to America. I want to go home."

Not me. America's fine, but this is where I feel at home. Guess I'm still a German at heart. I know why Papa went to America, making a living here was hard, but things are getting better. I'd stay in Germany if I could, but Mama and Katrina need me. My family comes first.

"C'mon," I said. "Get the cards. Oma and I challenge you to a game of Skat."

On the sail back to America we all stood at the ship's rail one evening after dinner. Gus said to Mama, loud enough for her to hear over the big ship's engines, "Trudy, I want you to know I'm impressed with how well you've organized starting the Camp, and this trip. And with the gentle, caring way you handle the children. I realize it's too soon to speak, but when you're ready, I hope our relationship can become more than employer and assistant ... even more than a friendship."

Trini and I looked at each other and grimaced, both wishing we weren't there to hear.

Mama clenched the deck rail, and, after a glance at us, replied, "I'm flattered, Gus. And you're correct, it is too soon."

Meanwhile, back in the States, Camp Klein's enrollment flourished. Every Sunday morning the new troop of a hundred or so uniformed campers paraded down Yarmouth's Main Street from the railroad station to the campground, marching and singing German songs. They carried the American flag and the Swastika, side by side.

After a morning of clearing land, we campers changed our clothes and marched to lunch. Then Gus usually gave a lecture about revamping American culture to operate more effectively, like that in the new Germany. Our afternoon activities were suited for each camper's age and gender. I was nearly fifteen, so I learned how to shoot a rifle and a Luger pistol, and how to use a trench knife, the standard close combat weapon for German Army Soldiers. My leader said I was a natural with the knife. Katrina's group of twelve-year-olds learned cooking, sewing, knitting, and childcare.

"I love wearing this uniform," I told Katrina. "It makes me feel like I'm a part of something important."

Starched white blouses with black neckerchiefs caught under the collar, and black skirts were the girls' uniform; we boys wore brown shirts, black neckties, black pants and a cap with a red Swastika.

But, Katrina didn't agree. "Except for the black beret that we wear on cool days, I can't stand this outfit. It's frumpy." The beret captured her thick flaxen braids, but she had the habit of flicking back the ringlets that framed her face.

Every Saturday afternoon the camp assembled for inspection by Gus and some visiting German Army officers. Eight-year-olds stood at the front of the gathering, progressing to the oldest campers at the rear. Gus swelled with pride as he looked over hundreds of children, ready to obey the commands of the *Fuhrer*.

"What a sight. Be proud of your accomplishment," he said to our camp leader. "This is the future of the Nazi cause. These are the soldiers who will rise up on *Der Tag*, 'The Day' Hitler will liberate America."

Every Saturday, Gus mounted the podium to address the crowd, saying, "Congratulations to the graduating campers today. You've done a splendid job, and you are a credit to Germany and to America. You will bring all you have learned here to share with your fellow students at home, as well as many educational materials to distribute. It is your duty to remind your parents to obey the *Fuhrer's* commands, and to promote solidarity by giving business only to those merchants who are pro-German. *Heil Hitler!*"

Katrina and I, and hundreds of other campers, raised our arms and voices in response, "*Heil Hitler*."

In the summer of 1938, Camp Klein's Board of Directors selected the five older boys they considered the brightest and most patriotic to visit the Reich Chancellery in Berlin, to see the German Army Officers in action. The board selected me. I thought it was a sure thing, but Mama was skeptical. She spoke to Gus as if I weren't even there. "After all, Heinrich already knows Berlin, he grew up there. And I don't want him missing three weeks of school."

"But it's an honor that Heinrich achieved all on his own, by his own merits." Gus leaned forward in his chair. "And even though he lived in Berlin as a child, he's never visited the government buildings. It would be educational."

She consented only after I pleaded, "Please, Mama, I'd really like to go."

Those three weeks changed my life. The army personnel treated us like visiting royalty, giving us free reign to explore the buildings. We watched history happening as German officers plotted strategies on huge wall maps to move soldiers forward into liberated territories. They made on the spot decisions affecting the progress of the war. It was a storybook world, like moving toy soldiers. But the officers had authority, the results were real, the decisions were life changing. It was hypnotic.

When I returned, I couldn't wait to tell Mama and Gus the details of the magnificent Reichskriegs Ministerium, with its huge marble columns and oak paneled offices, "big enough to hold a dance in," I guessed. "The soldiers' uniforms are swell, and they do serious work like reading maps and making plans for Germany's future. We didn't have a formal audience with the chancellor, but we met him in a hallway and were introduced."

He was smaller than I expected. Better not say that out loud to Gus. "He smiled at each of us and asked our names. Then we saluted him, face to face! And he gave us autographed photos as souvenirs."

My experience inspired me. It was exciting, and fun. It was swell. I hoped to convey all that to Mama, but instead of looking cheerful she frowned. Her eyes looked sad.

Camp Klein's success skyrocketed Gus's reputation nationwide. The Directors of the Bund Society elected him its national leader. Mama arranged speaking engagements for him at most of the country's sixty-five Bund organizations. Gus brought Mama's pamphlet, *Building Camp Klein*—with all the steps necessary to establish a youth camp—to Bunds in Chicago and Los Angeles. Newspapers and magazines interviewed him; articles were written about the camps he inspired. Gus became a celebrity. During his frequent trips away from the office anyone with a question or concern about the Beechwood Bund asked for Mama. She loved it.

Earlier, in 1937, a respected Bund member named Wolfgang "Wolf" Schlager had stood up at a meeting, shouting, "How about giving some of the other members here a chance to suggest activities? We have ideas too. This club is very one way! Your way!"

Everyone talked about the incident. It was a huge insult to Gus, a breach of club etiquette. The Bund was a democratic club, but everyone knew Gus ran things.

By all accounts Gus handled it well. Apparently, he bit his lip, smiled, and said, "Come to my office after the meeting and we'll discuss any ideas you may have, Wolf."

Wolf declined Gus's invitation. That week the Bund's Board of Directors ousted Wolf Schlager from the club. We never saw him again in America. But two years later, in Germany, Wolf told my friends and me that getting booted out of the club was a big favor. It motivated him to act on something he'd been thinking about for years. He redirected his anger and frustration at the Bund into the energy necessary to begin realizing his dream.

Germany's Defensive Surveillance System, DSS, functioned brilliantly at gathering intelligence. Wolf told us he'd itched to take the process a step further. "All the ammunition we needed to create a team of top-notch German saboteurs was gathered daily by DSS. I knew we could use their stockpiled information for real military advantage."

Wolf couldn't wait to get out of Beechwood after the Bund's action. He hustled back to Germany to campaign for his unique plan, explaining it in fine detail to anyone who would listen. After two years of prodding, he convinced the leader of DSS to fund his project. He set up shop on a farm just outside of Brandenburg.

The German military knew about Hitler's plan to invade America. Wolf wanted to be prepared. He contacted his old friend, the board chairman of the Beechwood Bund. "Franz, I need your help. I'd like the names and addresses of the five boys the Bund honored with a trip to Berlin. They'd be seniors now, and I'd like to extend an offer for them to work for me."

He contacted me and the four other Beechwood boys by special delivery letter on Reichskriegs stationery. *This must be a joke. But the heading looks authentic. What if it's real.* My hands shook. I held my breath as I opened the letter. After congratulations on my upcoming graduation, Wolf offered to pay me well if I would return to Germany for a secret Government position. I read the words three times ... "secret Government position." I felt lightheaded. I had to sit down and take a deep breath before I could continue reading

Wolf instructed that this letter must be for my eyes only, and must be destroyed whether I accepted or not. If I agreed to his offer, he would send details as to how I should proceed. It was the most exciting thing I'd ever experienced. Imagine me, working alongside the army officers at the Reichskreigs.

All five Beechwood boys in the class of '39 agreed to Wolf's offer. One cancelled a commitment for college to accept. He contacted each of us on the official stationery of a different United States company offering employment. Train tickets to different destinations, and a bonus for travel expenses were included in the package.

"But, Heinrich." Mama sat at the table, with that furrowed-brow expression again. "Dearborn, Michigan!

When did you decide to be a mechanic for the Ford Motor Company?"

"Mama, I did it on a lark, but I got the job. And look, $50 for my travel expenses. I'll be able to send some money back home for you and Katrina." I tried so hard to sound convincing.

Directly after graduation the four other Oakhill boys and I left on different days, with our families seeing us off at the train station. We made our way to New York Harbor, and met on board the SS *Bremen,* bound for Germany. To maintain normal communications with home, I was directed to send an envelope with letters addressed to Mama to a DSS member named Charlie at Ford in Dearborn. Charlie would then forward them to Beechwood with his own return address, and he'd send Mama's replies to Germany.

We met at an ancient farmhouse outside of Brandenburg. It had been empty for decades. Wolf renovated the kitchen with a huge gas stove for cooking and heat. He furnished it with two long wooden tables for our meals together. The kitchen had the only indoor plumbing in the house.

He and the instructors used the first floor rooms for meetings and relaxing. We students had the massive attic space for sleeping, and any private articles or books. "Your first duty, boys," our leader Klaus said, "is to dig three latrine trenches, and then build your own outhouses. Hans will direct and supervise you. Summer school focuses on fitness. Each of you must reach his personal physical peak in these first months. The tasks required to complete your missions will be strenuous."

"Hard to believe that I'm having fun digging this garden," Rolf said to me as we sweat through a sunny June day.

"Yeah." I plunged my spade into the lush soil again. "The kids in America are laying around at the beach, but this feels like real work, like it makes a difference." We ate nutrient rich foods and maintained a vigorous daily physical exercise routine. We felt invincible.

Sabotage classes started in October. Informants for DSS had infiltrated European and American airplane and automobile factories, the staffs of major newspapers, and even some military bases, establishing the foundation for Wolf's plan. We Brandenburg students were trained in extraordinary techniques for a new approach to sabotage. We must be fluent in at least one foreign language. Mine, of course, was American English. Then we learned the traditions, common expressions, and current popular music of that country, becoming fully familiar with its culture. I had lived in New York, but I learned some customs of the American southern states as well. Training included parachuting, camouflage techniques, several types of demolition methods, and map reading. Since we'd be working in life and death situations, we used live ammunition for our practice sessions. This was not a game.

We took field trips to German aluminum plants, railroads, and bridges to become familiar with our future targets. DSS provided photos and detailed drawings of the actual enemy sites. Our strategy was to infiltrate a community and blend into the daily fabric of life. We'd take all the time we needed to analyze our target, plan the most effective strategy for its destruction, and disappear when the deed was done. Scenarios were set up in which the expected plan went awry, forcing us to improvise. My education became second nature.

Unlike other German military groups, we represented a variety of races and nationalities, reflecting our target countries. We were intensely serious about lessons, but otherwise camp was informal. There was no heiling Hitler. We considered ourselves loyal German patriots.

"You're going to hear rampant propaganda about Germany's war efforts as you travel abroad to accomplish your missions," Wolf told us. "It's all lies. You must steel yourselves against it. But you must never expose yourselves to the enemy as German sympathizers by refuting it. Understand that using language as a weapon to attack our German Government is just as much a part of the war as using guns. We pride ourselves on our distinguished German heritage. Know that we are in the right whatever you may hear to the contrary by those who would destroy our Germany. Sometimes dignity is in stillness."

One of our classes addressed the possibility of capture. We memorized everything we learned in order to avoid paper evidence. German Army uniforms would be worn en-route to a strike. A saboteur faced a quick court-martial and execution, but a soldier in a German Army uniform would be taken prisoner and detained until the end of the war. A suicide pill was also standard issue. I would give my life for Germany, but could never take it myself, so I tossed the pill.

We were accountable to one man, the leader of DSS, but we responded to whichever German military service needed our skills. We became the Brandenburg Commandoes. "I've heard some rumors that the regular Army generals don't like our tactics," Rolf said to me. "They say we're 'unmilitary and devious'."

"Maybe we are, but we do what works. Let them look at what we did in Poland. We captured a strategic railroad tunnel and two thousand Polish prisoners of war. Can't say our first outing wasn't a huge success. Maybe they're jealous."

"Yeah!" Rolf clapped me on the back and we shared a grin, proud of our efforts.

Besides the German Army uniform in my duffle bag, I had a trench knife, Luger pistol, and explosive materials with time delay devices. I had a counterfeit birth certificate, Social Security card, draft deferment card, driver's license from America, and enough money in American bills to sustain me for months at a time. In my wallet I carried photos of myself with an American girl at the beach drinking Cokes.

My first year at Brandenburg I faced a challenge. How can I tell Mama and Trini I can't come home for Christmas?

I wrote, "I have to stay in Michigan for the holiday. I have some classes to attend." Part of it was true, but the classes were in Germany. I was sure Papa would be proud of me for being able to send money to Mama at Christmastime. I arranged my next trips to America so that I could spend a whole week at Christmas, and a few days every summer, with Mama and Katrina.

By the beginning of 1943, I had made several successful trips to America. Some of the "accidents" I caused were at a railroad bridge in Ohio, a hydroelectric plant in New York, and an aluminum plant in Chicago. I worked hard to be physically fit and mentally prepared, ready to fulfill my solemn Brandenburg vow to protect Germany with my life. In an award ceremony attended by all the Commandoes, Wolf presented me with a German Army Service Medal, a bright red oval with an eagle clutching a swastika. My efforts were acknowledged and appreciated. I had found my calling.

Before Germany declared war on America in 1941, I'd traveled there in comfort aboard ocean liners. But those crossings ceased with the start of the war. DSS then arranged for me to hitch rides on Scottish merchant ships to Canada, but the trip in 1943 would be my first ride on a German submarine, U-boat 636.

Two sailors met me and my travel mate, Johann, at the dock in Lorient, France, on July 2nd. German sailors hustled in all directions, rushing either to board a departing vessel, or to spend a few days of shore leave in the occupied city. One sailor picked up our gear to be loaded on the boat; the other sat us down on a bench against a building for a briefing. "I'm Kurt. I understand neither of you has ever been on a U-boat, so I'm going to tell you what to expect, and what we expect of you."

We introduced ourselves and then paid close attention to Kurt's instructions.

"First," Kurt referred to his checklist and then returned it to his vest pocket, "U-boats are submersibles, not submarines. We can travel undersea, but our engines, and the men, need fresh air. We used to travel on the surface during the daytime, got some sunshine, but those American planes are too good at finding us now. So, we travel undersea during the day, and surface at night.

"On the surface, we're powered by diesel engines. They're fast, but noisy. Get used to it, and avoid the fumes if you're on deck. The diesels charge the batteries that power us undersea. Then we move at a slower speed but batteries are quieter. It's a cycle. Get it?" We nodded, yes.

Reaching for the list, glancing, and replacing it in his pocket, he said, "Food. We have the best food available. We're fifty-six men with provisions for anywhere from six weeks to six months crammed into 115 feet of steel tube. So not an inch is wasted. You may have hams hanging from the ceiling over your bunks.

"Now, you guys are lucky," he said, placing a boot on the bench and towering over us, "You have your own bunks for the trip. The rest of us, except for the officers, share our bunks with a sailor whose duty hours are opposite ours. Once we leave port we're like a family ... respectful, but no saluting, and, except for Captain Erlich, we use only our first names."

He stood to continue his briefing. "As soon as we get into deep water today we'll do a test dive to be sure everything's in order. You'll hear a loud horn, and the captain will order over the loud speaker, 'Dive, dive, dive!' Whenever you hear that," he said, flipping his thumb for emphasis, "you get in your bunks and stay there ...

out of the way. Any interference with a sailor's duties, even for a few seconds, can be dangerous. Got that?"

Again, affirmative nods.

"Okay. Now, there's one toilet on board, so be quick. Never use it when we're undersea with enemy ships above. And, if we're running silent to avoid the enemy," he said, leaning over us again, "get in your bunk and make no sound ... don't even fart. Clear?"

"Right, yes." We nodded.

He stood to say, "You'll notice we have a water distillation system on board, but it only makes enough fresh water for cooking, drinking, and supplying the batteries. Do not get caught washing yourself or your clothes, or shaving, or even brushing your teeth with it, or you'll be punished. Once or twice on a patrol we can set up a saltwater shower. Otherwise we men just add to the worst problem on board ... the stench. So this is standard issue." He reached into his jacket pocket and gave each of us a tiny bottle of French cologne.

"Use it, or give it to your girlfriends. I don't care. Other smells on board come from some of the food spoiling. Rotten potatoes are the worst. Now, Captain Erlich runs this boat. We have the best captain in the service. He's like the best father a guy could have. So, I hope," he said grinning, "you boys are ready to see some action, because we'll find some. Any questions?"

"Where are the extra torpedoes stored?" I asked.

"Right under your bunk," Kurt said as he left chuckling.

We followed Kurt down the steep plank from the dock onto the wooden slatted deck of the boat, and through a hatch to the boat's interior. *Right now it smells pretty good here, like a spicy butcher shop.* Net bags of fresh produce hanging overhead assaulted us we stepped off the ladder. Some kind of food was stashed into every available nook. We found our bunks just where Kurt claimed, in the forward torpedo room.

As one of the sailors slid by, he informed us, "You'll have to fold up those bunks during combat in case we need more than the four torpedoes in the launching tubes."

I answered, "Yes sir. Thank you, sir."

"Name's Erich," the sailor said. "No sirs here."

"Forgot. Thanks, Erich."

We climbed into the bunks and Johann said, "Good thing there's a rail at the edge. It's so narrow I'd fall out the first night. How about exploring before we get underway?"

"Good idea."

To the clang of metal hatches closing, boots scraping on the deck, and sailors greeting mates after their leave, we made our way through the watertight hatch to the next compartment. Fortunately the bathroom was right there. Officer's and captain's quarters occupied the right side of the corridor with a curtain for privacy, and a row of huge batteries lined the left. Sailors skimmed past us going both ways getting ready to leave port. Next stop, the radio room. Some sailors wore headphones. Radar and sonar screens filled desks along an entire wall, and tables folded up along the opposite wall to create a conference area for officers.

The next hatch led to the control room, but we weren't confident enough to venture there in the frenzy of this moment, so we returned to the safe haven of our bunks. Immediately, Captain Erlich's voice boomed over the speakers, "All hands on deck for cast off!" Everyone, except Johann and I, jumped up and headed for the deck at the captain's words.

I chose to call the flippy feeling in my stomach excitement rather than anxiety before the test dive. But I enjoyed the sensation of slipping forward undersea.

"That was pretty smooth, huh Johann?"

Johann's white knuckles gripped the rail of his bunk across the way. "I'm happy to have it over with. Now at least I know what to expect."

I might have been more apprehensive if I'd known that the test dives began because the French resistance in Lorient had sabotaged some boats. But the test went well, and we surfaced to make headway west. Hearing the roar and clang of the diesels at full power made it clear why the speaker had to be so loud. *Should have brought earplugs.*

U-636 sailed along smoothly for the next few days with no storms or enemy ship sightings, giving us time to settle into our tight surroundings and meet the crew. They welcomed the new boys who hadn't yet heard their old jokes. We explored further aft to the control room with its dozens of valves, levers, and gauges. Two periscope masts extended through the conning tower in this command center of the boat. We found Captain Erlich there. I introduced myself and Johann, hoping we weren't out of bounds in our explorations.

"Not at all, boys. This is your home for the next few weeks. I trust Kurt gave you all the information you need to know."

"Yes. Thank you, Captain Erlich," we said in unison.

The next compartment housed the petty officer's quarters, with bunks for crew on the opposite wall. Through another hatch we entered the galley where the air became warmer and more smelly—like a mustardy barbecue sauce. *This kitchen is smaller than Mama's.* At tables against the wall sailors smoked, played cards, or read magazines. Others poured themselves cups of coffee.

"Hey, we got some new guys," one sailor said.

"No, we're just along for the ride. I'm Heinrich and this is Johann."

A sailor sitting on a bench at one of the tables said, "Welcome aboard your cruise ship. I'm Franz. Did Kurt give you the lowdown?"

"He did." Johann said, sliding alongside Franz. "He mentioned that Captain Erlich is quite well liked."

"And he deserves to be," said Franz with a nod. "There are some amazing stories about that man."

"Not stories—the truth," chimed in another sailor.

"What stories?" Johann asked.

"Well," Franz began, seeming eager to tell of his captain's exploits. "Back in early '42 Captain Erlich commanded a U-boat in the North Atlantic when radar spotted a big ship a few miles away. Now, by this time we'd already been fighting the English for three years. They defended their ships with armed destroyer escorts. Those little ships are fast. They gave us all kinds of trouble, still do. But the Americans hadn't learned that lesson yet."

"Not for another year after that," Erich said grinning.

"True," Franz said. He gathered the attention of more sailors. "Anyway, cruising on the surface was safer then, so the captain revved up those diesels to top speed and got a bit closer, then he submerged. At 800 meters away from the ship he rose to periscope depth, and to be sure, he saw no escorts. An American troop ship sailed out there all by herself. So our captain did his duty. He made his calculations, lined up his torpedoes and, as she came into his line of sight, fired all four. They all hit. That ship was going down," he said, gesturing toward the ocean floor with his thumb.

Everyone in the room listened to the familiar story as Franz continued a bit more softly, as if sharing a secret, "Through the periscope he could see lifeboats being lowered, and some US sailors were picking up survivors in the water. He saw a few guys manning the guns on the ship's deck. They left only when everyone had abandoned ship. Then, when the big ship started to sink bow first, Captain Erlich surfaced. He ordered his crew to join him on deck and directed the U-boat to draw up to the lifeboats." Franz paused.

"The crew, and probably the guys in the lifeboats, assumed that he would finish off the survivors so they couldn't disclose the U-boat's position to aircraft in the area. The captain approached the closest of the lifeboats and asked, in English, if they had fresh water. 'No,' the sailor answered. Captain Erlich ordered his crew to bring gallons of precious fresh water and food to the deck, and hand them down to the sailors in the lifeboats.

"Then the captain did something that amazed his crew. He stood at attention ... and so did the sailor in the first lifeboat. They saluted each other. Then Captain Erlich turned, ordered his men below deck, and, following them, gave the dive order."

Franz sat back with a grin, just as the captain entered the galley for lunch. "Telling that troop ship story again?" he asked. "It's not at all unusual. Many German U-boat captains aided survivors of ships they sank. Americans rescued U-boat survivors as well. I fulfilled my duty when I destroyed that weapon of war: the ship. She could never transport the enemy to Europe to fight Germans again. Look, we're all seamen, just doing our best to survive. Our duty is to sink ships, not to kill sailors. What's for lunch?"

When the captain went up to the kitchen counter, Erich confided to me that, "In the U-boat service your daily life depends on the character of your captain. They run their boats according to their own rules. We're lucky, we've got one of the best."

"I've heard a couple of times that it used to be safer for U-boats to be on the surface during the day than it is now. What changed?" I asked.

"Well, in '41 when the Americans entered the war they weren't trained to fight U-boats. And, as Franz said, they didn't borrow the British convoy system. They just let their ships roam about unprotected, so we picked them off easily. We were undetectable. I patrolled New York Harbor one night about a year ago and they didn't even turn off the lights, on the ships or on shore. They lit the way for us. We had no resistance."

"Yeah," Werner said. " We sank four hundred Allied ships in '42. At the start of the war Admiral Doenitz wanted a thousand U-boats built, not hundreds. We'd have dominated the Atlantic. But no one listened."

"Yeah, he was right," Erich said.

"But," Werner continued, "then the US Navy started using convoys and they developed that radar on their planes that can detect us five miles away. It's like magic. Changed everything."

"You just wait, Werner," Erich said. "Hitler himself is getting involved in regaining control of the Atlantic. He's ordered hundreds more U-boats to be built. And they have *snuiver,* that snorkel that'll let us get air while we're underwater."

"Too late." Werner shook his head. "To use the snorkel we have to stay at periscope depth. We can't use it, and sink ships, if we have to go deep to avoid those planes. Maybe a year ago more boats could have done serious damage. We lost our chance."

"Cheer up, boys." Captain Erlich slid onto a bench at the table with his lunch. "It's a game of one side finding new weapons, and the other finding defenses against it. Our turn's not over yet."

That day I signed up for a Skat tournament, and Johann, who loved to cook, volunteered to help in the kitchen. Three eight-hour shifts a day meant there were always sailors looking for a meal or a game of cards in the galley.

Next time we were undersea, Johann and I ventured into the diesel room. Those engines were gigantic, and the men servicing them were grimy from head to toe. This had to be one of the worst duties on board. Through the next hatch were the aft torpedo room and more crew bunks.

Since the boat surfaced only after dark I forgot what sunshine felt like, and the air in the boat became more pungent by the day. Sometimes fumes from the diesels seeped into the boat as it dove. The sailors seemed to bear the hardships of daily living with pride, as if to say, "This is a challenge, and I'm tough enough to endure it." I tried to shave without water, but it irritated my skin, so I let my beard grow. Not being able to shower bothered me. I've always kept myself and my clothes fastidiously clean. That would be the test of my patience on this trip.

On the sixth day of the patrol, the radio room sailors reported to Captain Erlich that our boat was ordered to join a Wolf Pack, a group of as many U-boats as could be mustered to destroy an enemy ship. Six boats were gathered. A British cargo ship, accompanied by a convoy of five destroyer escorts, had been spotted only a few miles from U-636. Radios were used as little as possible to keep the boats' positions from being discovered, but they did plan the combat strategy and responsibilities for each boat.

"Our first fight!" I said to Johann, butterflies fluttering in my belly. We abandoned our bunks, folded them up, and moved off to the galley in case the stored torpedoes would be needed.

"The Wolf Pack's only about 1000 meters from the target. Get set for some action!" a sailor said, rushing by the galley.

"Wish we could hear what's going on," Johann said.

"Be right back." I slid along the corridor from the galley into the back of the control room. The sailors of U-636 were an effective war machine as they synchronized equipment to make the necessary calculations. I bumped into Erich. "What's happening?"

"The destroyers have detected the Pack and started toward us. Five boats will engage the destroyers. Our boat will attack the cargo ship. The boys are calculating the speed and angle for the torpedoes. The speed of the ship, the angle of its bow, and the range from the boat determine those coordinates. The captain will situate us at a 90-degree angle to the ship, and we'll hit her bow to stern. She'll go down," he said.

Back in the galley I reported to Johann what I had learned. Then Captain Erlich's steady voice came over the intercom, "Torpedoes one and three, range 600 meters. Fire one. Fire three."

With a piercing hiss, the torpedoes propelled from the boat toward the big ship's forward hold. Five seconds later, two more were fired amidships. The first two torpedoes hit, sending shocking concussion waves surging through the sea. As U-boat 636 rolled side-to-side, lights blinking, Johann and I held onto the table bolted to the floor.

"What a ride!" Johann said.

"Hold on. We're not done yet."

U-636 stabilized and fired the last two torpedoes into the stern. Two more blasts reported hits. The last two hits insured that the ship would sink. The Wolf Pack dispersed and submerged for cover.

"We got three of their destroyers," a sailor bragged at the galley doorway. "They turned and limped away." The other two destroyers weren't finished with the U-boats. They chased the pack, launching a barrage of depth charges. U-boat sailors knew that the most dangerous explosion would be next to the hull, but undersea I noticed that every sailor looked up, waiting for a charge to hit.

Hearing the pings of a British destroyer's sonar bouncing off the hull, Captain Erlich took U-636 on a course in the opposite direction from the battle, and remained unscathed. When all had quieted down, the galley filled with sailors and tales of "That was close!" "We got the big one!" and "Good job, boys," from Captain Erlich.

Severe weather pre-empted any other maneuvers for the next few days. Our boat heaved and tossed like a child's toy through the rolling swells on the surface, the bow lifting then crashing into the black, icy waves. Some of the new ensigns learned about seasickness. Hammering rain soaked the sailors on bridge patrol at night. The musty smell and humidity of wet uniforms hanging to dry further degraded the nasty air inside the boat.

The first night the weather cleared, American planes found U-636 on the surface. The horn blasted and the captain gave the order, "Dive, Dive, Dive!" My heart raced as we ran to our bunks. "How can they find us in the middle of the Atlantic?" Johann asked.

"Aircraft carriers launch them." I scrambled into my bunk. "Franz said their long-range radar is designed 'specially to hunt U-boats. Once they find us, the pilots can send destroyers to our position, or they can fly over and bombard us with gunfire. If we'd stayed on the surface until the plane caught up with us we wouldn't have a chance. We can thank the captain for acting as soon as he saw the blip on radar."

This emergency dive was more like a roller coaster ride than the any of the previous dives, and much more strenuous for the crew to execute. The boat crash dived to 1000 meters, running silently on batteries.

During the next few days and nights of clear weather, American planes stalked U-636 like vultures. Our radar gave ample warning of the plane's approach, but because of the many dives the air in the boat deteriorated, as did the morale of some of the sailors. Finally, because the diesels had no time to replenish the batteries, our only defense was to dive and sit in silence on the bottom.

Johann bit his lip, and wrinkled his brow. "I hope we don't have to stay down here very long. We weren't surfaced long enough to get any fresh air. I can hardly breathe now."

"Best thing is to stay quiet, use as little oxygen as possible. The captain will get us out of this," I said, with a confidence I didn't feel. During a sabotage strike, I commanded every detail of the attack situation. Not here. I was totally out of control. My skin crawled.

Enemy planes were equipped with two lightweight bombs and several depth charges. Some charges exploded close enough to shake the boat. Sometimes a pipe connection loosened, causing a water spout that the sailors repaired without concern. No serious water leaks meant no damage to the hull.

We were trapped on the bottom, in a steel tube that couldn't move, being shaken by bomb's concussions. Johann's ashen face peered at mine for some answer to the dilemma, but I could only whisper, "Hold on." Anxious glances across the aisle between our bunks communicated more than any words could.

Then a depth charge scraped, metal on metal, along the boat's hull. Johann grabbed the rail of his bunk, assumed a fetal position, and whispered a prayer. But the charge never exploded. A dud. Three others did explode, but keeping silent must have worked because they missed by quite a distance. Meanwhile the air we breathed was nearly lethal. Johann became lethargic.

"Wake up, Johann," I whispered whenever I dared.

After an eternity of two hours the horn blasted and the captain announced, "Surface, surface, surface!"

I will never forget my first breath of fresh air when we reached the top. Better than any Christmas present I'd ever had. The experience with the planes sharpened my enthusiasm for this mission. I've never believed in coincidence. I was on my way to destroy a factory in Oakhill, Massachusetts, which produced both sonar for American ships and long-range radar for their planes. I couldn't tell anyone about the mission, not even Johann, but knowing it made me feel much more a part of this U-boat family.

Two weeks later, on August first at midnight, our boat stopped fifty yards from shore at Newport Beach, Maine. It was the night of the new moon, the darkest of the month. Steve, a DSS member from Massachusetts, rented a cottage on the shore for the weeks of the U-boat's August arrival and October pickup of two passengers. Only a few darkened cottages dotted the beach. Steve's lantern in the diamond shaped second floor window of his cottage shone like a beacon for U-636.

"Good luck, boys. Be here on October 28th at midnight." Captain Erlich gave each of us a handshake and a pat on the back. "We can wait only thirty minutes, so don't be late."

"Okay. We'll be here." We climbed down the ladder and jumped into the dinghy with Steve. Halfway to the beach, I stripped down to my shorts and dived into the cool, clean water to wash off the stink of the boat. After we each had a hot shower and shave at the cabin, Johann and I relaxed with a beer.

"I'll never again take fresh water and air for granted." I sipped my beer, grateful to be on dry land. "And those guys on 636 have another three months for this patrol."

"There's a rumor on the boat that their mission is to lay mines close to shore from Maine to Florida," Johann said. "But the best part is that the order came right from Hitler. Seems he's annoyed that the tide has turned, so to speak, for the U-boat service. They're getting sunk by the dozens and he wants to get the US aircraft carriers before they even get out to sea. That's how we happened to get the ride to America."

"I'll never forget the experience," I said. "Those guys are small in stature but huge in courage to be in that service. Once we get home my U-boat days will be over."

We were up before dawn to walk the quarter mile to the train station. Speaking English, we said, "See you October 28th. Good luck."

Johann headed north; I caught the train south toward Boston, which stopped at Oakhill. I bought the *Oakhill Chronicle*, rented a two-room apartment I found in the classifieds, and headed to the Salvation Army store for rumpled clothes an unemployed American man might wear. At the used car lot I bought a '39 Chevy coupe that showed its age, and took a ride for my first look at the factory.

After a quick lunch at the Oakhill Diner, I walked the few blocks down Main Street to the factory. Phil, the manager, grinned as he welcomed me, surprised to see an able-bodied young man applying for a job during wartime. After I filled out an application and showed my draft deferment card, Phil hired "Henry Miller" to do maintenance work starting the next day.

I made friends easily at work. They adopted me. "You look to be in pretty good shape," Bob the foreman said, implying, "how come you're not in the service?"

"Yeah, but I have flat feet. Didn't even know I had them until I tried to enlist. Otherwise I'd be overseas now."

I had the run of the factory. I gathered tools and equipment the workers needed, cut the grass in front of the building, and picked up packing materials from each bench at the end of the day.

I noted which aspects of the fabricating process were most critical, and which machines performed those tasks. I decided to use three explosive packages on each side of the main aisle connected with wire and attached to a delayed timing device. The scattered blast would effectively obliterate all stages of the process.

Once I planned my strategy, I judged when would be the best time to execute it. Severe afternoon thunderstorms were forecast for Monday, August 16th. Perfect. The cracks of thunder would camouflage the explosions, giving me extra time to disappear. On the 16th, I dressed in my black Commando uniform under the factory coveralls and shirt. Clearing all my things out of the apartment, I filled my duffle bag, and drove to work a few minutes early. I parked in my usual spot near the back of the building, and dug a hole in the tangle of sumac bushes there to hide the bag for later retrieval. With the necessary explosives stashed in my lunch pail, I buried the bag, checked that the window at the rear of the storage room was ajar, and went to work.

It took only a few minutes after quitting time to set up the explosive devices. Once they were in place, I rechecked each step of the process, and set the timer for ten minutes. Plenty of time to escape out the storage room window, retrieve the bag, and vanish.

Satisfied with my efforts, I turned the key to start the timer and pushed the bar to open the storage room door. A shiver went up my spine. I was not alone. The sound of children's laughter assaulted me.

3

Peter Pietrowski

America, 1933

In May, I drove my wife Gail and our three-month-old twin daughters Christine and Maria from Albany, New York, to Oakhill, Massachusetts, to buy a gas station and garage. For the previous three years I had worked in my father's garage every day after high school. My mother did the books. It was a family affair. No question about it, I'd work in dad's garage after graduation. I was a good mechanic. Regular customers requested me, saying, "I want the best mechanic in the place to work on my car. That'd be your boy, Peter, right?"

But after I started working full time, Dad and I argued constantly about the business. His garage was the only one on our side of the city. He had a monopoly on that market, but he refused to expand. On a certain

Thursday afternoon, we got into it hot and heavy. "I'm fine with my business the way it is." Dad wagged his finger at me. "You don't remember a few years ago when we weren't sure whether we'd have food on the table. I'm not risking what I've built up. And I'm sick and tired of you telling me how to run my garage." He turned his back and walked away, but I wasn't finished.

"You gave up before you even started! You can't see what's right outside your door. When some young sprout opens another garage down the street, and you can't compete, you'll lose the chance to expand. You're so thick headed!" I was shouting, frustrated. I threw the wrench I'd been clutching in my hand across the room, missing my father by inches.

"Okay, that's it, boy. I've had enough of your temper. When an employee throws something at me it's time to go. You're fired!"

"I quit!"

I found the garage for sale in the *Boston Globe* classifieds. It was in a renovated barn, with a rundown farmhouse on the property. Not exactly luxury, but perfect for our family. I bargained on the price as much as I dared, and demanded the owner include a few pieces of furniture in the sale. I paid more than I'd wanted to, using nearly all of our savings, but we had shelter and a business. The rest was up to us.

We had only a few possessions. With the old oak kitchen table, a few mismatched chairs, a rocker, and a couch that we bought with the house, we set up housekeeping. We splurged on a new bed and bureau for our room, some dishes, and enough kitchen utensils to start us off.

"We'll have to watch money real close," I told Gail after making our investment.

She looked up at me with a grin. "But in hard times, people will repair and keep their old cars and trucks rather than buy new, so when other businesses fail, ours will do well."

Setting up the shop was a joy. The previous owner had been a meticulous mechanic, maintaining the shop in much better condition than the house. When I stood in the garage, holding my case of tools, I felt like I was home. It was mine, to run my way.

No time to lose. I bought the forms for job tickets, worksheets, and invoices that Mom had used, and showed Gail how to fill them out. She set up her office in the dining room of the house. Then I visited the parts distributors in Boston to introduce myself and open accounts. I interviewed a dozen men looking for work, and hired one experienced mechanic and an apprentice. Regular customers of the last owner showed up right away, curious to see who bought their garage. We had work in the first few days.

I wasn't so mad at my dad that I didn't borrow some practices from his business that worked. For instance, I bought lunch for the mechanics every day. Better to treat them to a twenty-minute lunch break than to have them take an hour at the diner, and maybe have a couple of beers before coming back to work. I needed them clearheaded to get the jobs done.

The coffeepot was always hot, and I kept the fridge stocked with cokes for the men. I drove them hard to work carefully and fast. "Get the work out right the first time," I said. "You can relax after five."

And they did. At five o'clock, when they had cleaned the floor of grease, and the tools were put away, we stopped and pulled a couple of beers from the fridge. My garage became the spot for some of the hard-working men in town, or the local guys who were out of work, to get together in the afternoons. We'd talk sports, local news, or sometimes they'd even find out about jobs available and get some work. They didn't bother my mechanics during work hours. I wouldn't have it. But they were there at closing time for conversation and cool beers. If the Red Sox were playing we'd all gather around the radio and listen to the game, particularly when Lefty Grove pitched. I kept a cribbage board handy for a game or two.

Gail and I had a son Max the year after moving to Oakhill, and Paul was born three years later. Not long after starting the business I discovered I could make more money working on trucks than on cars, so I expanded and hired two more mechanics.

I couldn't stand sloppiness. I had rules at home as well as in the shop. I told Gail, "Dinner will be ready at six with my children, clean and happy, around the table, or there will be consequences." More often than not I might be late. A ball game, or some other distraction at the garage, could detain me. Even so, Gail and the children honored my rule. I was respected in my home.

Sometimes I had to scold my twin girls for being tardy or not helpful to their mother, but I never did hit them. Paul was either too little or too frail for punishment. His health was tender, like his mother's. And he was the spittin' image of her too, with the straight brown hair and dark eyes. By the time he was six he'd been in the hospital more'n four or five times, with some respiratory sickness. Gail said the nurses called him "an old soul" because he daydreamed, or read his books all day.

But Max was a big boy, built like me. Had my light hair and blue eyes too. He was tough. Even at nine-years-old, he could take it. To be sure that the other children benefited from my lessons about punctuality and respect, they were obliged to stay in the room.

4

The Boxes

Susan Miles looked out the kitchen window and saw Max Pietrowski smiling and swinging his arms as he walked up the hill toward her house with his little brother, Paul. Anyone could see that Paul idolized his big brother, and Max seemed to thrive on that admiration. Susan was an only child, but she played with the four Pietrowski kids so often they considered her one of the family. At her back door, she heard Max call, "Susan, c'mon out."

Through the screen Susan called, "Need to finish chores. A few more minutes."

When Susan went outside, Paul said, "Max showed me some of his secret marble moves. The ones he uses to win the big glassies." She noticed that while they waited for her, Max had polished the edge of the hole in the ground they used to play marbles to an exquisite smoothness. "Guess what, Sue. We found a secret place!"

"No kidding! How secret? Where is it?" she asked. The notion of a secret place captivated her. After the Roy Rogers Saturday matinee, the troupe of five neighborhood kids galloped, slapping thighs for sound effects, over the rocks and through the Wild West of their back yard hills. And they recreated Dracula's castle under the cobwebbed porch at Susan's back door. "Let's go!" she said. "Maybe there'll be ghosts or goblins for me to use when I write my next play."

Outside with her friends Susan felt free to express her natural enthusiasm and curiosity, but in her house she moved cautiously She felt safe only when her father was home. Her mother would never hit her when he was there.

Louise Miles could strike Susan as hard with biting words as with her hands. Susan could never get it right. And she could never figure out why. Whenever Louise was determined to teach her a lesson, she'd chase Susan into her room yelling the whole way that, "I'll give you the back of my hand."

And she did, repeatedly, as Susan huddled on her bed against the wall. *Wish I had a nickel for each time I made her mad at me. I'd be rich!*

Eventually Susan stopped trying to make sense of her mother's angry outbursts and just stayed out of her way, spending more time with her friends. In the fall, she found refuge at school. A whole day without yelling or hitting. She excelled there. But summer was tricky. Outside with her friends was the best place to be.

Max and Susan had been buddies since they were five, in first grade. At the beginning of this summer Susan complained to Max about the flimsy shorts girls had to wear. "This is 1943. Girls are doing all kinds of men's jobs, so why don't they have dungarees for girls?"

He went to Grant's with her and her mom to buy play clothes. "Let's go to the boy's department." He led them to the back of the store, and said to Louise, "Dungarees are the best. See? She won't get her knees so dirty or scraped. Size 10. Perfect for running through the back yard or kneeling on the ground to play marbles. And they cost less than shorts." He convinced her.

"Let's call for the twins too," Susan said as she and the boys passed Max's house on the way to the secret place.

Christine didn't hesitate. "Sure, show me!"

Her twin, Maria, trailed along. "I'll go as long as it's not buggy."

"Follow me!" Max shouted, assuming his position as leader of the group. The caravan of kids traipsed through backyards, trekked behind the movie theatre and the stores on Main Street, and headed for the old brick factory. Connected to the back of the building, cloaked by sumac canes and burdock bushes, stood an annex built of the same brick as the main building. Max surveyed his discovery, hands on hips. "Looks to be about wide enough to park two Ford pickups, and it's twice as deep. It's high too, goes up to the roof of the factory. And look, it's got extra windows all around the very top."

A grimy, double-hung window about six feet above the ground was their only access to see inside. "You have to stand on this rock to peek in the window," Max said. He avoided the burdocks, spread the sumac canes, and climbed up to demonstrate.

Christine scrambled onto the rock beside him. "I'm first. Wow! Wait'll you see this, Sue."

"My turn." Susan took Max's place on the rock, and, with a little lift from Christine, peered inside. Empty cardboard boxes of various sizes and shapes nearly filled the room. Susan found a crack of space at the bottom of the window, just big enough to slip fingers under. She lifted the rusty frame ... it moved. Shoving a little harder, she opened the window barely enough for a petite, nine-year-old child to squeeze through. "Boost me in," she said.

Max and Christine pushed on her butt and then her legs. Susan sat on the foot thick ledge of wall, took a deep breath, and hopped down onto the boxes. She crunched a few of them, and scrambled to her feet. Rather than shout over the banging noises of the factory machines, she motioned to Max to raise the window frame from the outside. He squeaked it open so Christine, who was tallest, could boost him, Maria, and Paul into the opening. Then he leaned out as far as he dared for Christine. "Pull on my arms." She ducked her head into the opening and scrambled up the outside wall until all five children were in the room.

Cardboard boxes filled the towering space to two feet below the window. They sloped to the floor, leaving three feet in front of the opposite wall bare. A ponderous metal door on that wall led to the factory. Shafts of light streamed into the room from the row of clearstory windows at the top of the three exterior annex walls.

The boxes moved underfoot. "It's like being on an icy boat deck in the middle of the ocean," Susan said. Max cautioned everyone to be quiet, but the grinding, clanking, and banging noises from the factory drowned out not only their voices, but also their squeals of, "Hey, watch this!"

Balance was critical. A box that looked stable might shift under some weight, creaking as it collapsed, but the empty cardboard containers afforded a soft landing. Maria and Paul stayed put once they found their footing. Max, Christine and Susan experimented to discover how much they could move around and remain upright. The worst that could happen seemed to be a scrape on the sharp edge of a box flap.

Once they found their sea legs, Susan and Max surveyed the room. Regardless of the whirring and clanging of the factory machines, the oppressive heat, or the musty smell, their imaginations created dramatic scenarios for their secret space. "Think of all the different places we can make out of these boxes," Max said.

"Yeah. Instead of running around outside all the time, we can be cowboys or pirates right here!"

"Who wants to play Guard the Castle?" Max asked.

Of course, he would be the King, and Susan the Queen. Christine played the Brave Knight, Maria the Lady in Waiting and Paul the Jester. They tore some of the smaller boxes apart to fabricate shields and crowns and found two sturdy boxes for thrones.

"We need swords," Christine said.

"And capes and combs," added Maria.

Clearly, they would have to bring equipment on the next visit.

"C'mon Christine." Maria tugged on her sister's shirt. "We'd better be home before five to help Mom with supper or we'll get it."

Christine helped Max out of the window first since he was strong enough to catch the other kids. She climbed out last. Then Max gently lowered the window to an almost closed position. "Better leave it open a little, for next time."

Most of the group of five kids played in their new hideout every day after chores. The worry that a worker could open the door from the factory at any moment heightened the drama of their fantasies. Since it didn't happen on the first few visits, it ceased to be a concern.

On a particular Monday afternoon they peered in the window to discover the boxes were gone. Nothing remained in the room except some frayed pieces of rope, a pile of sticks, and some discarded combs on the floor. "I'll bet they were collected for the war effort," Maria said. "Some ladies at Oakhill Center Grocery said that they were saving stuff to send to the troops."

"Don't know why they'd want our boxes." Max pouted at the sorry sight.

"Cheer up, Max," Susan said. "Maybe the factory will start collecting them again." And they did. The next day the floor and part of the window wall were covered.

Dramas created for the boxes demanded props, costumes, and one time a perfect mustache fashioned from the long hair of Max's dog's tail. Many scenarios were based on the Saturday afternoon movies. They never missed a matinee. On some Saturdays, when their parents deemed money for the movies too much of a luxury, Max got his wagon and they traveled the neighborhood, knocking on doors to collect old newspapers, or, even better, 2 cent returnable bottles. When they collected enough treasure to buy the eleven-cent ticket for each kid, and maybe some popcorn, Max called Jake, the junk man, to buy their stuff. Fantastic stories inspired by a double feature of western heroes, swashbucklers, or sometimes horrifying monsters, were played out in the boxes.

At the movies the kids learned about the war. United Newsreels of it played between the main features at every Saturday matinee. With stirring music in the background, the resonant voice of the announcer described how, in 1943, America was winning the war with few casualties, thousands of Axis prisoners, and major victories in places with strange names. The war was real in a place called Sicily, but in Oakhill it wasn't a critical part of the kids' lives.

Here it was more of a grown-up concern. When the neighbor ladies got together for coffee at Susan's house she sat near the counter, pretending to read while being glued to the conversation. She overheard somber exchanges about whose son had been killed or was missing in action. They spoke in whispers, as if it were all a secret.

Everyone knew that the gold stars hanging in windows meant they'd lost a boy in the war, but she didn't personally know anyone who'd been hurt. She knew about rationing, though. Gas rationing meant going for a ride on a Sunday afternoon wasn't possible anymore. Her dad had to be sure to have enough gas coupons to drive to his shop every day.

And she had a new job. Her mom gave her the white block of whatever-it-was with the bright orange pill, inside a cellophane wrap. She sat up on the counter and squeezed, pinched, and molded the block until the color was evenly distributed, looking like the pound of butter they could no longer buy.

Max's mother, Gail, planted a victory garden. "Feeding four children with those ration stamps is impossible," she told Louise Miles over coffee one day. Gail enlisted the kids to help with weeding by telling them it was patriotic, that they were doing their part for America to win the war, and they eagerly pitched in. Sometimes when Susan and Max wanted an afternoon snack they'd snitch a carrot, saying they were thinning them out.

Mr. O'Donnell, the air raid warden, did his part for the war effort. In his black helmet and coat he visited each house in the neighborhood, checking the blackout curtains everyone had to buy. "My duty" he said "is to make sure there's complete darkness outside during an air raid." The screech of the sirens at the beginning of each raid was scary, and during the raid the kids had to be indoors until the all clear whistle. But they knew the raids were practice, like the fire drills at school, when there never really was a fire.

Everyone sang the songs like "When Johnny comes Marching Home" and "Don't Sit Under the Apple Tree," but the war was more an idea than something real. Just like the old song said, it happened "Over There" ... until a steamy Monday afternoon on the 16th of August, when far-off thunder rumblings warned of an impending late afternoon storm.

"It's a perfect day for sailing a ship," Max said. "We'll be pirates looking for plunder, like Errol Flynn in *The Sea Hawk.*"

Paul found flags left over from the Fourth of July. They weren't black with skulls, but "Close enough," Max said. They taped three white pillowcase sails to broomstick masts and stuck them into three large boxes creating their pirate ship, *The Black Eagle*.

"Ahoy, mates! Batten down those hatches and trim the jib!" Captain Max said. "A big storm's comin' and we'd better be ready."

Sails were taken down to prepare for the storm, but a huge wave from too much moving around toppled Maria, Paul, and Susan into the ocean. Heroes, Max and Christine rescued them with great fanfare.

Abandoning the pirate ship, Max suggested his favorite game: Guard the Castle. The actors remained the same as last time, except Paul who wanted to be the Sentry. Capes, crowns, shields, swords, and scimitars appeared. Boxes were selected to build a Royal Room with thrones and a Dungeon with ropes. They designated a Necessary Room in the corner near the factory, as far as possible from the play area, as someone always had to pee at a critical moment in a game.

Paul guarded a pretend hill when suddenly he turned toward the Royal Room. He slipped a bit, but balanced fluidly, as he was now quite adept at managing the terrain.

"Enemy soldiers are coming!" he shouted to the Royals. "They're on horseback and they want a war!"

"Gather the arms," ordered the King, "and pull up the bridge over the moat!"

A blanket of dark clouds predicting the afternoon storm rolled over the neighborhood, snuffing out most of the daylight in the castle and transforming the boxes into a shadowy forest. Time to muster pretend arms and build a fort with large open boxes to climb into and hide. War preparations inside the room became more frenzied as the storm outside intensified. Whistling winds slapped sumac canes against the factory walls, and the strongest gusts rattled the window in its rusty frame.

"It's getting dark. They'll attack as soon as it's night," Christine said.

Far off slashes of lightning and growls of thunder were perfect pretend enemy's gunfire.

"I don't like this anymore. I'm scared." Maria's voice quivered. She headed for the window. "I want to go home *now* Christine, before it starts raining."

"Okay. I'll take you, but don't cry," Christine said. "I'll come back if I can," she said to the others as she helped Maria out of the window. A few moments later the only noises in the room were the howling wind and slashing rain. The factory machines were quiet. Quitting time.

Taking his station at the window, the sentry spun toward Susan and the king with the grave report that the horses were nearly upon them. In mid-sentence he slipped and disappeared under the box he had been standing on. He poked his head up, cap askew, and said, "Horses comin' Sire." He, Susan, and Max giggled, then laughed out loud as he looked more like the jester he had been than the sentry he was trying to be.

All that laughter made the Sentry want to pee, and he headed for the appropriate place. Max continued to make Susan laugh at the silliness of Paul's tumble. Suddenly, Paul shrieked, "No! Max help!"

"He must be hurt," Max said. "C'mon!"

He and Susan scrambled over the unforgiving boxes, expecting to find Paul bleeding, but they couldn't see him at all. Susan called his name ... no answer. When they spotted him they stopped short, breathless. Susan grabbed Max's arm.

Paul stood near the factory door. Crouched beside him was ... a man!

"It's okay." The man smiled at Paul. "No need to be afraid. I work here."

"What do you do?"

"I pick up the boxes in the factory and bring them to this room."

"So we can play?"

"That's right. Is anyone else here?"

The man's voice washed over Susan like warm honey. He was dressed in black. His dark hair, combed straight back from his forehead, made him look like Count Dracula. Her arms got goose bumps when he looked up at her. He asked in that same silky voice, "What are you kids doing here? Shouldn't you be home for supper by now?"

Standing tall, Max seemed to marshal every bit of courage he could gather and said, "We're playing a game. Wanna play?"

"Sure," the man said, smiling at Max and Susan. "What's the game?"

Heinrich Mueller remained calm. He had six more minutes before the bombs detonated. He heard his Brandenburg Commandant saying, "Leave no witnesses. Sabotage is rooted in secrecy and surprise."

This is War. These enemy witnesses must be silenced ... but they're children.

"We're playin' Guard the Castle," Max said. "You can be the Dragon in the tower."

"Okay." The man stood up and climbed over some boxes toward the children's play area, and the window that led to the parking lot. "But I have to get home for supper. How about you?"

"He's right," Max said. "We're already gonna get it for being late. Let's go."

They all began picking their way toward the window when a violent gust of wind roared past the building, followed by a rolling, thunderous crack. Through the window they watched the gnarled branches of an ancient blue spruce approach and crash against the annex, as if to consume it. The children jumped back, away from the window, but Heinrich rushed toward it and pushed against the frame. It wouldn't budge. He covered his eyes and smashed the pane with his elbow, but clearly he could never get through the tangle of branches outside.

Okay, I can't finesse my way out of the building and disappear, but there's a good chance I can survive the explosion. The walls are thick and the blasts are set to go off near the center of the factory. But, as soon as these children tell an adult about me, my mission here will be jeopardized.

"It's okay," Max said. "We can get out through the factory now. They've all gone home."

He bounced over the boxes toward the factory door and pulled down hard on the lever. Just as he heard the click of the door unlatching, Heinrich commanded, "Stop! Don't touch that door!"

Heinrich leapt over the boxes and seized Max from behind. He spun the boy around and held him with his left arm across Max's chest. Max thrashed and wriggled to get away. Heinrich reached down with his right hand and drew a dagger from its sheath in his boot. He showed it to Max and held it at his neck, ordering him to, "Stay still!"

Susan grabbed Paul's hand and pulled him closer to her. She heard someone shrieking, not realizing it was herself.

Two minutes left.

"Let me go!" Max struggled to break the man's grip

The point of the knife caught Max on the soft flesh under his chin. A trickle of crimson blood ran from the wound.

Heinrich's mind flashed to Captain Erlich and the story of the American troop ship. *Maybe destroying this weapon of war, the factory, accomplishes my mission. Maybe ...*

Max flung his arm against Heinrich's. The knife flew to the floor. Heinrich muttered something the children didn't understand, but it didn't matter, because in the next moment their world blew up.

Dazzling flashes of light and explosions loud as a hundred thunder cracks shook the building. They blasted the metal factory door open and off its hinges, propelling it onto Heinrich who fell on top of Max, both disappearing into the boxes.

Susan and Paul were flung back against the wall. Every muscle in Susan's body tensed. Her mind strained to make sense of what happened. Was it lightning? Like when it struck her house? No, this force didn't come from the storm outside. It came from inside the factory. An explosion. Could it be a bomb? Could the Germans really be coming like they warned us in school?

She bent down to look into Paul's face. "Are you okay? Are you hurt?"

Eyes wide with terror, he shook his head, *no.*

She could see only Max's arm and one leg sticking out from under the door. "Max! Max! Please be okay!"

Beside him in an instant, Susan discovered strength she didn't know she had and pulled on his arm. Paul grabbed a leg. They tugged and freed him from under the man. His body was limp, his face white. Susan gasped at his ghostly color and grabbed his arms to lift and support him. But in a moment Max shook his head and recovered his senses. He'd escaped with a few scrapes, a bump on his forehead, and the bloody cut under his chin. He swiped the back of his hand across his chin and looked at the man. "He's dead."

In a gap between the door and its supporting box Susan could see the man's head. A bloody flap of scalp and hair had been scraped away, exposing the shiny white bone of his skull. Fascinating. A dead person. She locked this image away for a future manuscript.

Max tugged on Susan's arm to make her move. "C'mon. We have to get out of here!"

Thick white smoke belched into the room from the open factory doorway. Max bent down toward the man. "Max, let's go! What are you doing?" Susan thought she heard him mutter something like, "Finders keepers."

Max took charge. "Cover your nose and stay low! Hold hands! Follow me!"

They crossed the factory doorway. Tongues of orange flame licked at the grease on the machines that were twisted and gnarled into fantastic shapes. Electrical connections on the walls crackled and flared like Fourth of July sparklers as the flames grabbed them. The heavy wooden workbenches were in splinters, but not yet alight. Glow from the fires on each side of the factory revealed an aisle down the center of the room toward the front door.

Susan squinted to protect her eyes from the stinging smoke, and tried not to breathe the acrid air. Hunching down, she covered her nose with one hand and held tightly to Paul with the other. They scrambled over debris until they reached the door. Max grabbed the heavy brass lock, turned hard, and pushed the door open. Kids and smoke tumbled out onto the walk in the torrential downpour. Not taking time to catch their breath, they stumbled, then ran from the factory as if the man were chasing them.

Fat raindrops stung Susan's arms and legs, soaking her in seconds. Bursts of lightning and cracks of thunder were continuous. Max got down on one knee and told Paul to "Hop on!"

He carried Paul piggy-back as he and Susan dashed down Chapman Street beside the factory. They darted behind the stores, stopping to catch their breath only when they reached the parking lot behind Auden's Gift Shop. Paul slid off Max's back, coughing uncontrollably.

"It's okay. We'll be home in a few minutes," Susan said, stroking the locks of wet hair from Paul's eyes. As the three huddled under the building's overhang the first fire engines, bells clanging and sirens blaring, flashed past on Main Street. Paul clung to Susan. "We have to tell our moms what happened."

"No!" Max said. "We'll get killed. We have to promise never to tell. This has to be our secret forever."

"But the man's dead," Paul whispered.

Max kneeled, looked into Paul's eyes and said softly, "We weren't supposed to be in there. What would we say? A man tried to get out of the factory, then it blew up? Who'd believe a crazy story like that from a bunch of kids? They'll say we've seen too many movies. Maybe we'd even get blamed for killing the man. We'll be in enough trouble for being late. We all have to swear never, ever, to tell anyone."

And, one by one, they did.

Susan felt lightheaded and nauseous as she climbed the steps to her back porch. Her mother started yelling before the screen door slammed shut, "Where have you been, how ungrateful to be so late for dinner, look at how filthy you are ..." On and on, until her father said, "That's enough, Louise. Let her get cleaned up."

Sometimes her mother's fury was scary, but today her father was home. Susan could be certain there would be no hitting. She didn't have to wonder about the scene next door. Through the open windows she could hear a kid wailing. Max Pietrowski was getting it.

She said nothing, washed up, pretended to eat dinner and, as soon as the dishes were done, went to her tiny room. She stripped to her underwear, hopped onto her bed, and started to read a funny book. But even Wonder Woman couldn't keep her awake. She fell into a deep sleep.

At 6:15 the telephone in the Miles' kitchen jangled. Their neighbor spread the news, "The factory's on fire!"

Susan's father left his newspaper on the table, grabbed an umbrella, and ran out into the downpour to see for himself. Mr. Wilson's factory was the major employer in town. Applicants waited, sometimes years, for a job to open up, knowing it would be steady, secure and well paid.

Mr. Miles stood with a group of neighbors behind the barriers of cones and tape that Oakhill Police had set up blocking off Main Street in front of the building, and for a hundred feet on either side of it. Smoke, thick as a white lamb's fleece, and greedy orange flames spewed from the old front door. Oakhill Firefighters in oversized yellow slickers and heavy tan boots sloshed through puddles. Their captain, competing with wind, rain, and rumbles of thunder, hollered, "Hook up those hoses! Hurry it up, boys!" They moved with surprising agility, dug in, and poured water into the merciless blaze.

No one tried to get closer. Heat and caustic fumes radiated across the street, smarting the rain soaked onlookers' cheeks and eyes. Explosions erupted inside the building as the fire unearthed volatile materials. The crackle of breaking glass heralded windows shattering. "I wonder if the walls will hold," a neighbor speculated. Some wept as the firestorm engulfed the factory.

After an hour the thunderstorm passed, and the sun shone again for the rest of a sultry summer evening. Firemen were still dousing stubborn cinders, and black smoke swirled from window openings, but the raging flames had been quenched. Lives were changed in that hour. A man standing behind Mr. Miles said, "I don't have a job anymore. A hundred families will be crushed by this disaster."

Setting up right in front of Mr. Miles' group, the WBZ Boston News reporter interviewed Oakhill's Fire Chief Crosby. "A bolt of lightning struck the building and ruptured a natural gas line that went into the factory, causing an explosion," Crosby said. "Grease and flammables inside fed the fire."

"Was the building a total loss?"

"No. The fire was stubborn, and the interior of the factory became fully engaged, but we arrived within minutes of the strike and contained the fire before it spread to the storage area."

"Were there any injuries?"

"There were three. Two of our Oakhill firemen were overcome with smoke inhalation. They were brought to St. Michael's Hospital where they're being treated. One person in the storage room sustained serious injuries and was taken to Mass. General Hospital in Boston."

5

Heinrich's Journey

Where *am I? What happened to me? Am I dead? It's dark. Can't open my eyes. Can't move ... anything! Beeps, I hear beeps. And a voice, someone's talking ...*

"Hi Doctor Frasier. This patient was admitted today at 6:23 p.m. He was in a factory explosion at about 5:15, so he's been comatose almost two hours so far as we can determine. His chief injury is a skull fracture, and possible intracranial hemorrhage. Other conditions are a broken left femur, hip, and tibia, a double nasal fracture, left cheekbone fracture, and a fractured left clavicle. And his breathing is erratic."

Hey! I'm here. I can hear you guys. Talk to me.

"The emergency treatment has been oxygen, IV with antibiotics, glucose, and fluids for hydration. You'll notice his BP and pulse are elevated since being admitted, not a good thing for a guy who's bleeding in his head. He has no motor or verbal responses, and no eye movement. I'd say his condition is deteriorating."

Whoa! That doesn't sound good. Help me!

"I agree. Get OR One ready for emergency surgery. His odds for survival are slim to none. He's young, that's in his favor, but if he's to have any chance at all we've got to stop that bleeding and relieve the pressure. What's his name?"

"Henry Miller. He had a wallet with thirty dollars cash, a photo of himself and a girl, and a Mass. driver's license. The medic said he worked at the factory, so we'll be able to track down more information from his employer."

"Nurse Lahey, prepare this man for surgery, then have him transported to OR One.

A nurse. Okay, I'm in a hospital. Those voices were talking about me. Slim chance! No!

Hey, I felt that! A stick in my arm. Whoa ... I'm swimming in this black lake, beeps fading, voices gone, calm. I can see ... bright colors. I can move. And listen, I can talk. This is real. I'm swimming in the colors. The king and queen are swimming with me. I see their paper crowns. But they're leaving. Wait, don't go away. Beeps are coming back. Colors fading. Blackness again. Pain! An awful pain on my left side, and my head. Nurse! Can't you hear me screaming?

"BP and pulse are normal. Doctor, I've noticed a facial grimace."

"Thank you, Nurse Lahey. That's just an automatic response. He's not doing it consciously."

I am! I hurt! How can I tell you! Pay attention!

"Bathe and shave him tomorrow morning. We'll set his fractures and repair his facial injuries then. Good-night, Nurse."

Aha. I'm to have a bath. When they brush my teeth, I'll bite. Or when they shave me, I'll grimace again, so they'll know it's on purpose.

"Good morning, Mr. Miller. How about a bath?"

That's the same nurse. I hear metal clanging. She must have a container of some kind. Hey, that tickles. Oh, I'm getting a shave. Easy, girl. I think she nicked me.

There goes the sheet, and my gown's down over my arms. Oh, that feels so good. Warm, soapy water. Okay, now I'll just move my shoulders a twitch, just enough to get her attention. Damn! She's fast.

Moving legs now. Look at those thigh muscles jump, Nurse Lahey. And see me wiggle my toes! What? No! Not done already!

Nothing ... I could do nothing. I felt every touch, every movement, but I'm trapped in my body. I want to cry, but I can't even do that.

"I'm going to give you an injection."

Good. That world is much better than this one.

"Hi, Dr. Frasier. Got some more information about Henry Miller. He lives in an apartment building in Oakhill. He was deferred from the draft with flat feet, but his employer had no other information. Perhaps he'll have a visitor, and we can find out more about him."

That's all you need to know. No visitors, no questions, just help me wake up!

···❖···

How long have I been here? Will this be my world forever? Wait, a new voice.

"Okay, students, gather 'round. This patient was admitted with an intracranial hemorrhage. He's been in a coma for three weeks. He won't wake up. A week in coma causes irreversible brain damage."

Nein! Whoa ... speak English, Henry. I'll show you, ya jerk! I'll wake up. I'll beat this thing. I'll prove you wrong, fool. Every day when they move my arms and legs, I'll think about moving them myself. What it used to feel like. I'll will myself better.

"Calling Doctor Frasier. Wanted in Room 104."

"What's the problem, Nurse Lahey?"

"No problem at all. Look, Doctor. Henry Miller's eyes are open."

Blurry. I see shapes. Gray, white. A face. Coming closer. Bright light.

"Hello, Henry. Welcome back. Can you see my light? A good sign, Nurse. His pupils respond to light. Let's be vigilant for other signs of consciousness. It'll happen slowly if it happens at all."

For a while I slid in and out between coma and reality. When I was conscious I couldn't pin things down, everything moved too fast, confusing me. I just wanted to go back to sleep. I heard them say I had seizures.

I still couldn't move my arms or legs, and I couldn't speak words, but I could turn my head and before long I could make sounds that communicated what I did and didn't want.

Every moment I was awake a nurse or doctor asked me questions or poked a light into my eyes. It was maddening. I squirmed as much as I could to make them go away. Sometimes, before I became fully awake I couldn't feel anything. But the more alert I became, the more I drowned in a sea of pain. Then they started asking me to move my right hand or leg. That scared me because I had to think very hard about which was my right side. But with effort I actually could move. It was exhausting. Sometimes I yelled at them to leave me alone, but they didn't understand. They continued testing, and I continued improving. I wished that jerk with his students would come by again so I could show him I was awake, and tell him off.

In time I got some words back and passed the test for being out of coma by making "clearly conscious responses," but I had moments when I couldn't remember easy things, like my age. I'd take time, remember what year I was born and try to figure it out. Other times every object in the room became a different color geometric shape. Then I'd sleep a while and wake up feeling in a fog. They told me I'd survived the worst.

One thing I did remember. I would miss my boat ride on October 28th. There'd be no hero's return to Germany. In fact, I could never face returning to Brandenburg after failing my mission so miserably. My fault for being weak, not able to eliminate the witnesses of my strike. But I also blamed them for interfering with my plan. Except for the delay those children caused I'd have escaped unharmed, proceeded to my next target, and completed my mission.

Then I had a visitor. Mr. Wilson, the owner of the factory, came to see me and give me some "good news." Through my haze I heard, "You don't have to worry about any of your medical expenses. The factory has an excellent insurance policy. Since you were hurt in the performance of your job, your recovery will be covered until the doctors sign off that you're well."

I tried a "Thank you," reeling under the realization that no one suspected me of wrongdoing. *I'm safe.* I fell back to sleep.

After three months of critical care I regained halting speech and limited movement. "We attribute your recovery to your excellent physical condition at the time of the accident, Henry," Doctor Frazier said.

Although I exhibited what they called "agitation and cranky behavior," I moved from Mass. General to a rehabilitation center on Boston's south shore. My fractures had healed well, but I experienced some level of discomfort every waking moment. The persistent symptom which did not subside was generalized pain on the left side of my body. Physical therapy seemed to aggravate the soreness, but I learned to walk normally with a cane. Therapists told me strong painkillers would impede my recovery, so I could take only aspirin.

Every time I let myself dwell on the events of that August day I wanted to hit someone or break something.

The doctors called it "acting out," my way of relieving tension. I had survived. I would regain my strength and my skills, and, as long as they live, I vowed to find those children again. There is an old German saying, *mann sieht sich zweimal im leben* ... you always meet twice in life. Yes, those children and I would meet a second time, but with a much different result.

I assumed someone must have found my duffle bag by now, although I'd hid it well. With $15,000 in American bills, if someone found it they probably wouldn't say a word. When I'm stronger I'll go back to look for it.

I called Mama. "Heinrich, I'm so glad to hear from you." Then she wept. Hearing her voice again, I did too. "We couldn't find you," she said. "Our letters were returned, and no one at Ford knew where you were. Are you all right?"

"I served in the military, Mama," I said, not mentioning which country I fought for. "I've been injured, but I'm getting better. I'm at a rehab facility near Boston now, but don't think about visiting. I can't see anyone yet. Please let Trini know I'm okay. When I can leave here I'll come home to Beechwood. It's so good to talk to you, Mama. Can't wait to see you. I'll keep in touch. By the way, my name is Henry Miller now."

After six months of grueling physical and cognitive therapy, I could walk with a cane and carry on my half of a conversation, although I spoke more slowly than before. In June I boarded a train for New York, then switched to the Long Island Railroad and Beechwood, so grateful to be back with Mama.

I politely refused neighbors' invitations to talk about my time in the service, as many other veterans also did. Neighbors welcomed me home to the Beechwood community as a wounded American soldier. "We're so pleased that Heinrich, I mean Henry, is home at last. He's a lucky boy to have survived his war injuries," one neighbor said.

"What he needs now is his mama's good food and our loving care," said another. "He's such a charming boy, and so courageous. Imagine how he must suffer with those injuries, but they don't stop him from getting around. We need to show him how much we appreciate his service to America."

I continued the intense speech and physical therapy prescribed by my doctors, but I needed a diversion. Beechwood High School's Adult Education Program offered classes in creative writing and art appreciation. It surprised me to discover how passionate I could be about literature and art. Both my teachers became mentors, suggesting lists of books for me to read, and introducing me to New York's Morrow Museum of Art Seminars. Each month for a year I received a portfolio focusing on a particular group of artists with prints of their paintings, biographies, and a synopsis of each painting style. I devoured each one, teaching myself the variety of painting techniques that have evolved through history, and the artists representing them.

Researching ways to ease my constant pain without taking pills, I discovered meditation. I joined a group learning the ancient technique of mindfulness.

When I entered the meditation center I thought, *I'm in the wrong place.* A huge statue of Buddha sat in the corner of the room, and pillows were arranged on the floor, obviously for sitting on. With my hip problem I wouldn't be able to get up if I sat on one. I started to leave, but then an angel in a long white summer dress floated by and stopped me.

"I noticed you use a cane," she said. "Many of our visitors use a chair instead of the pillows if it's more comfortable. Here, let's find one for you. By the way, Buddha is here only to show us the proper posture. Ours is not a religious center. My name is Lila. Welcome."

I'd have followed her anywhere. She was the most beautiful and serene woman I'd ever seen. The instructor entered the room, smiled, and began to direct us in the correct posture and attitude for meditation. "No one can meditate wrong," he said. "Even if your thoughts make you stray from concentrating on your breath, that's expected. Observe the thoughts, dismiss them, and go back to focusing on the breath. The more you practice the easier it will become."

I was skeptical. This seemed too easy. But at the end of the hour I felt relaxed, alert, and happy. *Unbelievable.*

I wanted more of this calmness. After learning that Lila led the walking meditation, I registered for that session as well. It happened in the backyard of the center with its plantings and rambling stone walks. The pace was deliberately slow so that we could focus on and feel every part of our foot touching the stone surface, and, with our eyes lowered, we could experience the glorious variety of plants along the way.

Lila invited me to have tea at the end of the first session, and it became our practice. She was light-hearted and cheerful, her laugh like the tinkling of bells. Her positive attitude toward experiencing every aspect of life captured me. In a few weeks I admitted my feelings for her, and couldn't control my grin as she responded that she believed it would be, "natural for us to be together."

Lila and I were married in October, 1945. She continued her work at the Meditation Center and I found a job at *New York City News*, first as a copyeditor, then as a reporter with the arts and entertainment team. I reviewed new books and covered openings of new galleries. Our son Jeffrey was born the next year. I was living the American dream, with a house in the suburbs, a devoted family, and two weeks a summer on Cape Cod.

The persistent pain in my left hip never let me forget the incident at the factory. I hated being a victim of my indecision, and of those meddling children, but after being on the brink of death, I was grateful for my good life. I accepted the pain as punishment for my weakness. Whenever I let myself dwell on my missed hero's return to Germany, I became enraged. Periodically, and privately, I released tension on the nearest objects in front of me.

For fourteen years I believed I dealt with my problems, until the day George at *City News* brought a new poetry book called *Echoes* into my office. "Hey Henry. Here's the Poetry Association winner for '58.

Lucky kid," he said, looking at the photo on the back flap of the book. I took the book, glanced at the photo, and froze. *He's familiar*. Reading the introductory notes I came to, "...lives with his mother in Oakhill, Massachusetts." It's the kid from the factory, the littlest one. So he lived to win an award. Let's see how bad this book is.

The first poem I read called "The Ballad of The Black Knight" exposed me. *That brat is writing about me*. At the end of the ballad, the sentry rises up and slays the knight who had transformed into a black dragon, warning,

"Beware, ye' devils of the dark,
Who sin among good men.
Ye'r evil always falls to light,
Ye know not where or when."

6

Max Pietrowski

After the August 16th explosion at the factory, I helped out in my dad's garage every day. Anyone might think the violent experience Susan and I shared would bond us even closer, but we kept our distance for the few weeks left of the summer. I think we wanted to try to forget that awful day. At least I did.

But my body refused to let go of the experience. My terrors happened in the middle of any dream, any night, and were always the same. I'd be enclosed in a room that became increasingly smaller, crushing me until I couldn't breathe. I'd wake sweating, gasping for air, my body shaking, trying but unable to scream. Paul shared my bedroom. He'd wake up and try to comfort me, or at least calm me down. Each time he suggested calling Mom I refused, making him promise he would, "Tell no one."

One time after a nightmare, Paul gave me a silver medal the nurses at St. Michael's Hospital had given to him. "This is to keep you safe from your bad dreams."

Tears of gratitude rolled down my cheeks.

I continued helping out in the garage through middle and high school except when football practice interfered. Dad took pride in my success on the playing field, attending all the games, and forgiving work for practice. "I'll be so proud when I can add '& Son' to the sign 'Peter's Garage' after you graduate," he said.

At the beginning of my junior year at Oakhill High, my dad died. Instantly. Driving his truck home from work at about ten o'clock on a rainy night just before Halloween, he sped off the road failing to make the curve at Summer Street. He careened into a light pole, crashing it down onto the truck. Wet leaves made the pavement as slippery as ice, and the lack of skid marks showed that Dad hadn't even tried to control the speeding truck.

"He never saw the curve," the medic said.

Mom fainted on hearing the news. Neighbors came by to help, and afterward she tried to maintain her composure and dignity, "For the sake of my children," she said. "He wasn't perfect, but then who is? He had a temper, but he also had a big heart, and courageous spirit. He was my husband, and I can't imagine living without him."

My dad died. I knew I should have felt sad, grief-stricken. But I didn't. I felt free, relieved, like a burden had been lifted from my life. What kind of vile person am I? I never even cried at losing my own father. A few weeks after the funeral, Mom asked, "Max, would you like to take over your father's garage after you graduate?"

"No, Mom. I just worked there to help out. I want to go to college to study history and become a teacher."

Before that, I had never told Mom, or anyone, of my ambition. It was a dream, beyond my reach. My mentor in high school was George Gideon, the smartest, funniest, most caring man I'd ever met. I couldn't get enough of his knowledge of American history. He seemed to know things about people in the past that you'd only know if you were there. He made those people real to me and to all his students.

I often stayed after class to clear up a point he'd made, and the conversation sometimes got around to my life, and my plans after graduation. He insisted I should go to college, and helped me fill out scholarship applications, even though, at the time, I was positive I'd never use them.

Then my dad died. When I told my mother what I wanted she said, "That's exactly what you'll do." She sold the garage and I was accepted at Boston College, majoring in history. Mom offered me the option of living at school, "to grasp the complete college experience," she said. But because of the nightmares, I thanked her and said I preferred to commute as a day student.

At the beginning of sophomore year I had my first panic attack. Crunched into a booth with four friends, I was having lunch in the Commons when, out of the blue, I experienced an intense dread of being trapped. I couldn't catch my breath, my heart raced, I became hot and sweaty. *I must be going crazy or having a heart attack.* To avoid embarrassment I excused myself, and began to make my way out of the Commons. That's when I met Katherine.

A girl appeared at my side reassuring me that I'd be okay. She led me to a chair at a corner table, dumped out the bag carrying her lunch and, scrunching the top, told me to breathe in and out of it. Slowly my anxiety dissipated. She sat with me for at least fifteen minutes, introducing herself as Katherine O'Brien, a student at BC's Connell School of Nursing. When I could speak, I asked how she knew what to do.

"My Dad has panic attacks, so I recognized the symptoms right away."

"Oh, that's not what this is. I just got a little dizzy."

"Okay. Well, glad I could help. Here's my number in case you'd like to have coffee sometime." Katherine wrote on the paper bag, and she was gone.

The experience rattled me. My body had not behaved normally. I was out of control. I'd be sure to avoid crowded situations in the future. Through my next class I kept remembering Katherine with her dark brown hair, blue eyes, and dimples, surprised that I had noticed so many details about her. After two days I retrieved the paper bag from the back of my notebook and called the number.

"Hi Katherine. This is Max, the guy you rescued in the Commons. I wondered if you'd like to go to a movie Saturday night?"

"Hi, Max. Well, maybe. What kind of movies do you like?"

"Gene Kelly and Debbie Reynolds are in *Singin' in the Rain* at the Lowe's. It's a musical." I started to worry that she wouldn't go, and realized I really wanted her to.

"Sounds great. I love musicals," she said.

I picked Katherine up at her house and met her parents. I was always a bit shy meeting new adults, which seemed to make them feel more comfortable. With my Polish name the O'Briens would be sure I was Catholic, making them like me even more.

It wasn't raining on the way home from the movie, but Katherine and I started singing the title song. I amused her by "dancing" on and off the sidewalk curb, and swinging around a lamppost just like Gene Kelly did. I relaxed and we enjoyed each other's company. From that first night we were inseparable. I consumed my studies, especially the history of America. On a sunny spring day during our junior year, Katherine and I sat in the Commons, talking about our future.

"But how can we afford to get married and stay in school?" Katherine asked.

I scribbled the numbers on the package back of the Hostess Cupcakes we had shared, but they didn't tally out, and neither of us was willing to leave school and get a job. We had to wait.

The summer after graduation we were married in St. Ignatius Church on BC's campus. I was hired to teach American history at Oakhill High School, and Katherine began working at St. Michael's Hospital, just down the street.

My nightmares subsided after my marriage, but the panic attacks increased in number and severity. They occurred either in our house or my office since that's where I spent most of my time. I made a list of places to avoid that might trigger an attack including crowds, bridges, elevators—anywhere I couldn't escape. Almost everywhere. But I kept my childhood vow. I never shared what I believed to be the driving force behind my panic, the incident in the boxes, with anyone, not even Katherine.

We worked out a system for me to be able to work comfortably. First, I asked Albert Jones, the Athletic Director, "Hey, Albie, how about trading offices with me? I don't need all the space in mine, but I'd like to be right off the parking lot."

"Good deal," he said.

His office had its own exterior door. I could drive from my house to school, having to be outside only to walk up the stairs from the car to the building. No stops or diversions. Once I entered the school, if I noticed any discomfort, at a meeting, for instance, I quickly excused myself.

I dreaded having an attack in a public place, so I missed Oakhill High's Graduation ceremonies. "It's sad that I can't see my students graduate," I said to Katherine.

"I know, honey. We'll do something fun that day to take your mind off it."

I needed Katherine's presence increasingly more often. "I have to be at Town Meeting, to vote, to do research at Oakhill Library for my classes. And it's stressful being alone in the house, but I can't leave it."

Katherine's 3:00 to 11:00 p.m. shift at the hospital was constantly being switched or interrupted to accommodate my needs. Since I made twice what she did in salary, we decided she would leave her job to be available to me. To cut down on expenses we sold Katherine's car. If she needed to use the car during the day, she'd drive me to work and pick me up. That happened so often that, after a while, I stopped driving altogether.

For the next several years, Katherine became my constant companion and support. Her presence kept me comfortable. We were careful to avoid my triggers, but I could attend a party or family gathering for a few minutes if she was beside me. When she was driving I could ride in the car as long as she didn't try to cross a bridge. Our system seemed to work.

My condition developed into full-blown agoraphobia. Any public space became a threat, but Katherine and I managed to keep our secret. I tried to maintain my composure, but sometimes I lost it.

"I hate this! Most of my life is a lie. I want to smash this devil inside me. It's keeping me from living my life. I'm shackled. I'm not a free man!" Sweeping my fist across the kitchen table one day I knocked over a vase of tulips, breaking the glass and splattering the water. Recalling my father's vicious temper, I forced myself to swallow my feelings. *I will not be like my father*. His behavior toward me had been indefensible, based on the flawed belief that it was discipline. It was not the way any father should treat a son, but in that moment I did begin to understand how constant frustration could lead to irrational behavior. I neither condoned his offenses, nor absolved him of responsibility for them. But I understood his intentions, distorted though they were, and I felt free from the hostility and anger I had held. I allowed myself to be grateful that we had time to share the pleasure of my football success. The weight of my resentment towards him was lifted from my soul that day. I wept at the loss of my father.

Although Katherine and I were together constantly, except for my time at school, the fun and intimacy faded from our marriage. I found refuge in my classroom, especially when my students responded to my teaching. I gave every bit of creativity and energy I had to making sure they understood not only the events of their history, but also the people making the decisions that resulted in those events.

"Besides the materials prescribed by the school's curriculum," I told them, "I'm assigning each of you a biography to share with the class. You may choose from a long list of statesmen, musicians, poets and writers of the time we're studying. I call it Performing Knowledge, putting your knowledge to work to teach your fellow students.

"You may choose your method of presentation. Some of you may give a report, some may make a model, and some may perform a concert. Decide on a method that will clearly express your ideas for your classmates. I'll make extra office hours for anyone needing help with this assignment."

My goal was to help them discover that the people who made choices affecting our democracy were just like us, leading difficult lives and coping. I wanted them to see that they could get involved and make a difference.

Hoping to regain some of the closeness that had waned in our marriage, I suggested to Katherine, "Honey, you're such a caring person. We're great together, but one thing missing from our life is a child. I think you'd be a terrific mother."

"Max," Katherine said, "I have all I can do to keep up with our life as it is. We're fine, just the two of us. If you'd get some medication it might help with your problem. Maybe then we could talk about it, but not now."

"You know how I feel about medication. I have to be on my toes for my students. I'll try to find a therapist who works with people like me. I'll call St. Michael's tomorrow."

7

Henry Miller's New Job

"Henry!" Gil called from his office. "C'mon in here!" When I entered the office, Gil closed the door. *Uh-oh. I must have done something wrong.*

"Henry, how'd you like to live in the country?" Without taking a breath, he said, "I'll explain. See, *City News* has purchased a paper in Massachusetts, and we need a transition person to make sure it's operating as well as we do here. Now, I'll be honest, I offered the job to Frank first since he has seniority, but he has kids and grandkids here, and his wife won't consider moving from the city. We've been wanting this paper for a long time. It's next only to the *Boston Globe* in readership. You'll get a good pay raise, and we'll support you if you need time before moving. Once you move there, you'll be Managing Editor. Whaddya say?"

"Wow. Sounds like a great opportunity, but I'll have to talk to Lila, and Jeffrey has more than two years left before he graduates from Beechwood High."

"Perfect. Take the time to polish up the operation, then Jeffrey will be in college. We'll set you up in an apartment there, and you can commute weekends. You'll have time to explore the town, pick out where you want to live. And the North Shore is the up and coming place to be in Mass."

"It's Friday afternoon. Let me talk with Lila over the weekend, and I'll give you my answer on Monday morning. Where is it?"

"Oakhill. Right on the B & M Train line to Boston. Very convenient location."

I didn't hear anything after the word "Oakhill." My stomach churned and my knees buckled. I grabbed the corner of Gil's desk hoping my reaction couldn't be detected in my face. Swallowing hard, I said, "Hey, thanks for the offer, Gil. I'm glad to hear you have that kind of confidence in me. Monday morning, okay?"

"You bet. It's a good deal, buddy."

I used the time on the train ride home to meditate. I needed to bring my anxiety level down before seeing Lila. I knew she would sense my tension. I wanted to pose the offer to her as calmly as possible, without influencing her reaction. I still believed there were no coincidences. Fate gave me this opportunity.

She surprised me. As soon as I told her of Gil's offer, she smiled. "What an opportunity for you. To manage your own paper with the support of *City News*. And, I've just heard about a new Meditation

Center in Cambridge, Massachusetts. Imagine, a peaceful oasis in the heart of a bustling city. As soon as Joseph told me about it I experienced a strong desire to visit. We can give Jeffery a choice, but I think you're correct that he will want to graduate with his friends at Beechwood. He's doing so well I wouldn't want to interrupt his progress. I see a new door opening for us. How do you feel about it?"

How did I feel about it? On the surface I had no reason not to accept the offer of a significant promotion. But I needed to consider aspects of the move not apparent to anyone else. I'd been careful to leave no evidence behind in the Oakhill apartment, the factory, or the car, but I couldn't dig up my bag. Did the poet find it? If he did the threat in the poem was real. I'd be exposed. Then I'd lose everything.

But, if the poet has the bag with explosives, the phony documents, and a German Army uniform, why am I still free? Maybe the kid kept the money and got rid of the rest of it. Too many variables.

Recovering the bag loomed as a significant reason to return. I had to find it, or find out if the poet had it. The time had come to resolve the questions left behind in Oakhill. If the other children in the factory survived the blast, they've probably moved away. And if they haven't moved? Maybe I can be clever enough to deal them a blow they'll never forget ... and finally finish my mission.

The more I thought about it, the more comfortable I became with the notion of returning to Oakhill. My body had been broken, but I remembered the vigorous, skillful weapon of war I had been at Brandenburg. My training would support me in Oakhill, but there would be a more sophisticated outcome for my mission. Not like our operations during the war. My targets would know who did the damage, but be powerless to retaliate. I wanted them to suffer even a fraction of what they caused me to suffer every day. And I could take my time. They won't recognize me immediately because of the plastic surgery. Fate gave me this chance for retribution.

What if some old timer remembered my name from 1943? I'd admit being that poor kid who was nearly killed in the factory lightning strike, and now I was just trying to do my job. How could I not go?

On the day I gathered my papers to leave for Oakhill I glanced at the *Chronicle* information packet. Walking into Gil's office I said, "Pretty sure the address for the paper here is wrong, Gil."

"Let's see. Yup, 652 Main Street, Oakhill, Mass. is correct. Good luck Henry, and thanks for taking on this responsibility. I really appreciate it and I know you'll do a great job. You deserve this promotion."

With an arm around my shoulder Gil walked me to the office door saying, "Call as often as you can. I'm here for you whenever you need me. Anytime. See you in a couple of weeks."

Closing my briefcase I left the office. *No! It's impossible. Real life doesn't happen the way it does in books. I destroyed that building. I know I did. The town must have changed the numbers.*

For the entire drive to Massachusetts I couldn't stop thinking about 652 Main Street. I dreaded seeing, yet couldn't wait to see what was there.

Hey. Looks like it had plastic surgery ... like me.

The building had been restored to its original stature, with massive front windows and a covered entrance. The old oak door still had the brass lockset, though I noticed a modern keyhole above it. The staff expected me, welcoming me as I entered the brightly lit office. People were busily typing away.

I'm always excited by the buzz of a newspaper office. There's nothing like the staccato rhythm of the typewriters, people checking facts, moving their pieces to copyeditors for polish, with a deadline looming over every moment. Everyone in that office was obligated to get the paper to the breakfast table, or the newsstand, or wherever *Chronicle* customers expected their daily paper would be waiting for them.

My office sat at the back of the room, on an exterior wall with plenty of natural light. A mahogany desk, a brown leather desk chair, and four leather-upholstered chairs for visitors furnished the space. Half walls with windows at the top granted me a view of the entire outer office. Gleaming mahogany bookshelves filled the lower walls. *Yes, this will do.*

I could find no flaws with the redesign of the building when I took my first tour. I did reorganize the desks so that teams were clustered together making it easier for reporters to consult with their peers. The office became like neighborhoods of Arts and

Entertainment, Crime and Fire, Community affairs, and National News.

At the back of the office space a short corridor with restrooms on the left and a tiny kitchen on the right led to the door of the print room. As soon as I passed through it I could see that the wall to the old storage room was still intact. I approached the new metal door, pushed on the horizontal bar, and gasped. I couldn't catch my breath. Halting and leaning on my cane, I blamed my quirky hip for the hesitant stumble as I entered the paper's distribution room.

A ten-foot wide overhead door for loading the papers onto trucks and a three-foot wide exterior door replaced the window on the back wall. Outside, a canopy extended eight feet from the building the entire width of it to protect the workers and papers from the weather. A small platform and concrete stairs ran from the exterior door on the right side of the loading dock to the ground. No sumac or burdock bushes were visible, but I could pinpoint just where my duffle bag might still be buried, under the concrete stairs.

I contemplated retrieving the bag. I'd need the help of a child to crawl into the confined space. No, I'll take my time, analyze the situation, and devise the most effective plan. Rushing might jeopardize my long-term goal.

This is not a case of eliminating witnesses. Killing a person causes pain once, briefly. But ruining a person's reputation kills his spirit. It destroys his stature among peers, diminishes his opportunities for employment, and damages his family's trust in him. It takes time, but it causes pain repeatedly. Yes,

I'll act deliberately. That's the route I'll take for this operation.

I spent the next several weeks reviewing years of past *Chronicle* spreadsheets, interviewing staff members to become familiar with the newspaper's family, and planning how to make the paper operate more effectively. In a few months, I joined the Oakhill Chamber of Commerce, attending most of their functions, and was invited to become a member of the Rotary Club.

I offered the local non-profit organizations free space in the paper to advertise their fundraising events. I stood in the cold outside Oakhill Center Grocery ringing a bell and holding a red bucket for the Salvation Army at Christmas. I wove myself into the colorful tapestry of the community leaders, the active people in town who worked more with their minds than with their hands, but were always willing to roll up their sleeves to do good works. I became recognized and valued as a beneficial citizen of Oakhill.

I'd been at the *Chronicle* about a year when one of the reporters approached my office. "Come in, Bob. What can I do for you?"

"I thought you'd be interested to see this notice from the American Poetry Association, Mr. Miller. A local boy who won the Award in '58 is going to be on the *Today Show* with Dave Garroway next week. You know how he likes to promote writers. It's a young man named Paul Pietrowski. He wrote a book of poems called *Echoes*."

"Yes, I've read it. Thank you, Bob. How about getting an interview with him? We can talk about the book and get an article with a photo for the Saturday edition before the show. This is even more than local interest."

"Thanks, Mr. Miller. I'll set up the interview at his place on Craggy Pond, the 'Artist at Home' kind of thing. And I'll take Joe, he's the best photographer. Since you've read the book, what do you think *Echoes* means?"

"I'd guess it means memories. That'll be a good question to ask the author."

"Joe can take some great photos of the pond too," Bob said. "The views up there are amazing. I'll get on it right away."

Perfect. Let's see how the poet explains the content of his book. And I'll have precise photos of where his house is and what it looks like. The puzzle falls together.

At the Chamber of Commerce Annual Dinner, I made sure I spoke to Maria Pietrowski. "Hi. How's the beauty business going?" I asked. "I'm Henry Miller of the *Chronicle*. I recognized you from your ad in the paper. Clever to include a photo of yourself. Makes the ad personal."

"Thanks. It's my co-worker's idea and it does help. Customers feel they know me as soon as they enter the salon. Business is good. People always want to look their best, and once they visit the salon they come back."

"Say, are you related to Paul Pietrowski, the poet? I read his book. It's very creative."

"He's my little brother. We're so proud of him. Creative is a good word for it. I don't know where he gets those stories. He has a vivid imagination."

"You said 'we'. Do you have other family in town?"

"I do. My sister Christine is here, busy raising her family, and my brother Max is a teacher at the high school. He got some of those creative genes as well. The kids love his classes."

"Hey, your glass is empty, let me get you another white wine. Where are you sitting?"

"Thanks, but one's my limit. Anyway, my co-workers just walked in. I should go meet them. Nice talking to you."

"You too," I replied. "Good luck for the coming year."

I don't think she's the little pigtailed girl at the factory. No nerves at all, even when I mentioned the book. I struck out this time.

The next morning I looked through the files of the paper until I found the photo of the American history teacher, Max Pietrowski, with the group of new Oakhill teachers in September, 1955. That's my boy. His blond curls are cut short, and the fireplug body has lengthened and filled out, but I'll bet that kid has a scar under his chin. Be patient, the way will appear.

Two weeks later the eldest member of Oakhill's School Board, Ethan Blake, announced his retirement with two more years left on his term. The position didn't attract many citizens. The board spent months debating the school budget, inevitably ending with a sum higher than the taxpayers wanted to pay. It was a thankless job. No other applicants applied to fill the rest of the term.

I returned to the files to find Maria's sister Christine. She's raising a family, so her name is different, but I'll bet she had an engagement announcement in the paper. Probably in '50 or '51. When I found the photo of Christine Pietrowski with her long blonde hair, I knew she couldn't be the one. *So, who is the mystery girl child I encountered in the factory?* I savored chasing the solution to that puzzle.

8

Susan Miles

Christine greeted me at the front door of her bungalow with a big grin and a hug, obstructed by her bulging belly. "Susan. It's so good to see you. Welcome home."

"Thanks, Chris. It's good to be back home. Oakhill never changes. Everything's so familiar and comfortable here."

At that moment two identical towheaded four-year-old boys bounded from the back of the house. "Hello, hello, Auntie Susan!"

"Oh, so I'm an auntie now. I like that."

"This is John junior. Since his dad's always been Jack, we call him by his proper name. And this is Max. You know who he's named after. Everyone told me the twins thing skipped a generation, but here's living proof that's a myth," Christine said, walking me into the kitchen. "How's your dad doing?"

The scent of brewing coffee lured me to sit down at the table. "Fine, thanks. I intended to stay with him for a week after Mom's funeral, but it's been over two weeks now, and I don't want to go back to Chicago. So many sad memories there."

Christine busied herself with getting a plate of homemade cookies and two mugs of streaming coffee on the table.

"I've just rented an apartment over on Pleasant Street," I said. "It's half the second floor in one of the old houses. It has a sitting room, kitchen, and bedroom that could all fit into your living room. But it suits me now, like a little den to curl up in. I'm going to stay here for a while. Dad wants me to stay."

"We all do," Christine said.

After giving each boy an oatmeal cookie, still warm from the oven, Christine suggested, "Build something for Auntie Susan with your Lincoln Logs. Let us know when it's done." Settling into a chair, she said, "Annie's in school now. She's seven, and I'm due in October. This house will be bulging at the seams."

"How's Jack doing with the new business?" I asked, munching on the warm, sweet softness of an oatmeal cookie.

"Great. He's a meticulous carpenter," Christine said, pouring cream into her cup. "He pays such great attention to detail that people will even wait for him to do a job. He's the best dad, and the most gentle man I've ever met." Grasping the mug with both hands and raising the creamy liquid, she took a first delicious sip.

"Unlike your father." As soon as I said it I hoped I wasn't opening old wounds, but her response calmed my fear.

"Yeah, he was a troubled person. Add that to the drinking in the garage every day, and it had to end badly. After he died in the truck crash, we worried about Mom, but she got her driver's license and a job at Grant's. I'm so proud of her. And I'm lucky to have Jack." She tucked a wisp of flaxen hair behind her ear.

"It's not luck. You're smart. I'll admit, Jim Stevens wasn't my ideal man when I married him, but I believed I was in love. I never thought my marriage would fail after only six years."

"Fail! Not so, Susan. The man's an alcoholic. You don't need that kind of grief in your life."

"I know that now." I picked up my cup and took a sip, savoring the coffee aroma and taking that moment to gather my thoughts. "But I did love being married. He didn't drink every day at first. I had no idea how to handle it when he did. Finally I realized it was his problem to handle, not mine.

"I did adore having someone there who cared for me, until he chose to care for the beer more than me. And, I love kids, but I'm glad we didn't have any. This would be even harder. So, tell me," I said, ready for a happier subject. "What's little Paul up to?"

"Little Paul is six feet tall and still skinny as a beanpole," Christine said with a grin, offering Susan another cookie. "He's had some problems, but some good luck too. Actually, he's as close to being famous as anyone in Oakhill gets."

"Really? What'd he do?" I asked, choosing chocolate chip with walnuts.

"Well, remember how often he was in the hospital as a kid? So little and so sick. The nurses adored him. To thank them for their care, he wrote poetry for them. He called the poems 'Nurses' Verses'. More coffee?" she asked, getting up for the pot and filling my cup. "They gave him a little silver medal of Saint Nicholas, the patron saint of children, to keep him well and safe."

"We're done, we're done!" two identical voices shouted as the boys bounded into the kitchen. "You have to come see Auntie Susan."

"How about one more cookie while Auntie Susan finishes her coffee, and then we'll come into the playroom."

Deal accepted, John suggested, "Let's make Play Dough people," as they trotted down the hallway.

"Anyway," Christine said, sliding her bulkiness back into the chair, "Paul's still writing poetry, and at St. Michael's Rehab Center a few years ago, some of the nurses convinced him to let them send a packet of his poems to The American Poetry Association. They honor young poets whose first volume hasn't been published yet. They publish the poems, distribute the book, and award the winner a $10,000 cash prize. And he won. He used the prize money to buy some land at Craggy Pond and built himself a cabin there."

"That's terrific. I'll have to visit and congratulate him. Yummy cookies, Chris."

"Thanks. I have lots of practice making only two kinds. About visiting Paul, you might want to wait a while. Maybe Max can go with you. Paul's a bit under the weather right now.

"I'd like Max to visit with me. I haven't seen him since I've been back. He had a cold and couldn't come to my mother's funeral, but he must be okay by now."

"I'm so proud of my brother Max," Christine said. "He's a beautiful man, inside and out. His kids at the high school love him. They call him Mr. Ski. Guess what he does ... it reminds me of the boxes."

At that moment the phone rang. I was rescued from Christine detecting the blush that spread over my face at the mention of the boxes. I've never been able to lie, and that incident is the only subject that I can't tell the whole truth about. Besides the heat rushing to my face, my tummy flips whenever I'm reminded about the day of the fire.

"Okay, honey," Christine said. "I'll save your dinner in the oven, bye."

I looked up, attentive and grateful for the few minutes to recover. "One of the negative things about being so popular," Christine said, "is that Jack's schedule is full. Guess it's going to rain tomorrow, so he has to work late tonight closing in an addition.

"But about Max. Once a year he tells the kids that he won't be in school the next day, but they'll have a sub who has read the homework, so don't think they can skip it. Then he'll show up to class in character. He's been George Washington, Thomas Jefferson ... he picks tall guys like himself. And the kids can ask any questions they want. How's that for bringing history to life? Anyway, his most daring character was Eleanor Roosevelt."

"No kidding."

"Yes. And the kids were great. Of course, she's almost six feet tall, she wears loosely fitting clothes, and has that distinctive voice. He said they asked questions about her childhood and were sympathetic when she told them that both her parents died before she was ten."

"Yeah, I read somewhere she was born into wealth, but had a difficult childhood. It was an interview where she said her teachers influenced her the most growing up. And everyone knows how she worked to get safer conditions for factory workers."

"Right, and when Max's kids asked her about President Roosevelt, she said she advised him on matters concerning women's rights and education. And he listened to her."

"Yeah, sometimes I think she had more influence on him than any of us knows."

"Maybe. Well, then Max told them a little known story about a night when Amelia Earhart visited the White House for a dinner in her honor."

"Oh, I've never heard that one. Tell me more," I said, finishing my coffee.

"Well, it seems Amelia asked Eleanor if she'd like to go for a ride. Never one to reject an offer of adventure, Eleanor accepted. They snuck out of the White House and Amelia flew her in a little plane over the DC area for half an hour. They returned to find that no one had missed them."

"What does that say about the men of that generation? I mean, here are two brilliant women, but they're invisible. Eleanor never got recognition for her contributions until lately. Makes me wonder how much we don't know about what happens in the White House. Wish I could be a fly on the wall for a day."

"Me too. Anyway, when Max told me about the class, he said that up to that point all the people who had subbed for him were men, and he wanted to give the girls someone to cheer for."

"That was an incredibly courageous thing to do."

"You'll see him at the class reunion next week," Christine said. "And you'll get to meet Katherine."

"Now, what is it in your tone of voice that makes me skeptical about meeting Katherine?"

"Nothing really. She's sweet, and Max is devoted to her. It's just that, she doesn't let him out of her sight. She's so protective of him, like he's her kid. And don't mention kids. Last time I asked when they'd make me an aunt she left the room in a huff."

"Thanks for the warning. But I'm not going to the reunion."

"Of course you are," Christine said, picking up the mugs and empty cookie dish. "You loved high school.

All that work you did on the school paper and the yearbook, and you were voted, what, Cutest *and* Most Likely to Succeed?"

"That's the point. I've failed at everything in the ten years since graduating in '51. Not just my marriage, but everyone expected me be to be a writer by now, and I haven't written anything I can put my name on. I don't even have any good ideas. I was so cocky then. How can I face those people?"

"They're your friends. It'll be just like high school again when you see them."

"I don't know. I mean, when I went to Chicago with Jim I thought if I worked as an independent copyeditor I'd have time to write, but I had to work for five publishers to make any money. It was exhausting. Anyway, I don't have anything to wear to a reunion."

"That's not a problem. You're just about Maria's size, and she has closets full of clothes. You had so many good friends in high school. You have to go. And don't be so hard on yourself. You just haven't hit your stride yet. Hang around here for a while where people care for you, take life easier. The ideas will come."

We heard them giggling as John and Max raced down the hall and bounced into the room, gleefully clutching my hands to take me to see their construction. "Wait'll you see, Auntie Susan. We built a castle for you," John said.

"And you can be the queen," Max added.

An image of the castle the Pietrowski kids and I built at the boxes flashed across my mind. Most of the days there were good, carefree days. No disappointments, insecurities, failures. Only freedom and imagination then, just like the four year olds dragging me to their playroom.

"You go see the construction. I'll call Maria," Christine said.

A boy held each of my hands as we entered the sunny playroom. "This is the most creative castle I've ever seen," I said. The structure of green logs did form a box, with a plastic dinosaur on top. "What's the animal?"

"That's the dragon," John said.

"He's a good dragon," Max added.

"Thank you both. I love it," I said, hugging the squealing boys, "and who are the people?"

"That's Uncle Max. He's the king," John said. "And you can be the queen."

After lunch, Christine, the boys, and I walked the half mile to Maria's beauty salon in downtown Oakhill. "It's amazing that nothing much has changed here since I left. I mean, that grocery store was Ralph's and now it's Pioneer, but it's still there. And I can smell the bread from the bakery two doors away. Is the movie theater still operating?"

"It is. Remember the Saturday matinees? We had so much fun when we were kids at the movies, and the boxes, except for the fire, of course. Maria and I were terrified that day. We knew you, Max, and Paul were in the building. We didn't know what to do at first. We had just started to tell Mom to get you, when Max and Paul came through the door. We were so relieved to see them, and to hear you were safe."

"Thanks to Max. He got us out of there before the fire got too bad. I'll never forget going through the smoke. By the way, did you notice what the boys built for me? A castle! Made me remember the fun we had at the boxes. We never considered that we shouldn't have been there, did we? It was just our hideout."

"Well, the factory's one thing that has changed. Doesn't it look great? The Berkeleys did a wonderful restoration. Good thing, because it's so close to the center of town. You'd never know it was an old, burnt out factory at one time.

"Here we are," Christine said. "Maria has become quite the businesswoman. Her whole focus is on this shop. She loves it."

Manikins in stylish clothing, one with a long hairdo and one short, dressed the two windows at the facade of Maria's shop. Against a black background, a selection of colorful barrettes, combs and scarves decorated the floor and back walls. *Very classy.*

Inside, we were greeted with the fresh, clean scent of natural shampoo. Tables with magazines, two black couches with white toss pillows, and a row of coat hooks filled the waiting area in front of the desk. Four stations with black chairs and counters occupied the rest of the space. The back wall was painted mauve, the color on the cover of the current *Vogue* magazine. Technicians with clients occupied two of the four stations. One girl sat in her chair with a magazine, seeming to wait for her client. Maria stood at the reception desk in a little black dress, her chestnut curls cascading to her shoulders. "Susan! Welcome to Maria's."

"Congratulations. This is so nice."

"C'mon up to my apartment. Sandy, will you watch the desk?"

Maria led the group to the back of the salon and up a flight of stairs. She opened the door to a light-flooded room with a tranquil, understated elegance. A few upholstered pieces in plain woven fabrics of muted grays and tans were the only furniture. The green fronds of some floor plants and a large aquarium against the wall offered splashes of color. The only sound was the tinkling of aerated water being restored to the tank. A pair of brilliant blue and silver angelfish swam among a variety of plants. "Except for my fish," Maria said, "I like to be the most colorful thing in my space. This is where I wind down. I'm talking all day with clients, on the phone or at my station, so I come up here to be calm. It's my retreat."

"It's lovely," I said.

"Let's find you a dress."

Maria opened the door to the smaller of the two bedrooms in the apartment. It looked like a miniature department store. Cabinets organized one wall with hanging space for coats and dresses, shorter units housed skirts and blouses, cubbyholes held folded sweaters and tee shirts, and floor to ceiling shelves stored shoes. At the front window stood a full-length three-way mirror. In the middle of the room a Victorian table displayed dozens of hair ornaments and scarves.

Maria pulled out a pale green chiffon dress that looked as if it had just stepped out of *The Great Gatsby*. "This will be wonderful on you with your green eyes."

I tried it on and felt delightfully girly. Maria picked out some creamy colored shoes, and everything fit. "This is so sweet of you. Thank you Maria."

"It's my pleasure. Come by at three on Saturday afternoon and I'll do your hair. We can't have you wearing it in that ponytail."

On Saturday I closed my eyes, tipped my head back, and allowed myself to be pampered as Maria shampooed and coiffed my long brunette hair.

"I know the style is for a shorter cut now," I said, "but this suits me."

"It does, and that's what's important. We're both rebels, but you're a braver one than I am. That reminds me, I often think of how lucky you and the boys were to get out of the factory when the lightning struck that day. Can you believe we even broke in there? We're all lucky we didn't get caught."

"We are. My dad and I went to the diner for supper the other night and I noticed the factory building still looks great after the renovation."

"Yeah, it does. The older people in the Chamber tell me that the building caused some contention in town for a while."

"Really?" I said, shouting over the whirr of the hair dryer. "Well, I remember it was empty and ugly for two years. Windows were all boarded up, and no one was sure if the thing might fall down. I was too scared to even go near it."

"I guess that's when the merchants on Main Street took up a petition to have it torn down," Maria said. "But, just before the wrecking ball came, the Berkeley family bought the building to house the *Chronicle* there. I heard they picked it up at a bargain, but then they gutted the inside and restored it.

"The paper's been running out of it for years. But recently, when the third generation of Berkeleys should have taken over, they wanted no part of the newspaper business. That's when the matriarch, Mrs. Howard Berkeley, decided to sell. She comes in here every week to get her hair done, so I hear all the gossip."

"Who bought the paper?"

"Some New York newspaper company. Mrs. Berkeley says it's the best move she ever made because the kids have no talent for journalism and would have run it into the ground.

"There. How's that?" Maria asked, standing back with a satisfied grin. My hair curled softly at the ends. A silver clip held it back from my face.

"Amazing. It looks so pretty, Maria. I think I've found a new hairstyle. Thank you."

"Well, if anyone asks where you had it done, you can tell them here."

The "Ten Year" banners and red and white balloons were festive, but no matter how the Reunion Committee tried to disguise it, I detected the familiar leathery smell of Oakhill's High School Gym. A twitter happened in my stomach as I walked through the door ... I bumped into Max. The loose blond curls I remembered were closely cropped and had darkened to light brown, and he'd filled out with muscle in the last ten years, but those familiar sapphire blue eyes captured me. I saw the adventurous nine-year-old boy from my childhood. A warm glow flowed over me. I had missed my friend.

"Susan," he said, "I'm so glad to see you. This is my wife, Katherine."

She is adorable. Look at those dimples, and deep blue eyes. They'd have gorgeous kids. Better not say that.

"So nice to meet you, Katherine."

Just then three of the people who worked with me on the school newspaper came up with greetings and hugs. Christine was right. Seeing them again transported me back to high school, like no time had passed. I was swept into the crowd until I noticed Max and Katherine leaving. I went to say goodbye, and to Max said, "Let's get together for lunch so we can catch up. I'll call you."

"Great," he said as they walked out the door. Funny, they left before dinner. Must have had another place to go.

The rest of my evening was the most fun I'd had in years.

The next Wednesday I called Max at work and invited him to come to my apartment for lunch.

"Can't," he replied. "I have to stay here, but can you come to my office? How about tomorrow?"

"I'll bring lunch," I said, and showed up at his office the next day with sandwiches, apple pie wedges, and coffee. Shelves of books covered nearly every inch of wall space in the tiny office. An overstuffed chair welcomed guests. "This is very convenient, right off the parking lot, and it feels so comfy."

"Yeah. I always get a parking spot, and the kids don't feel like they've been called to the office when they're here."

"Katherine seems very nice."

"She is. She's indispensable to me."

Indispensable. Interesting word for a spouse. Stop it, Susan. The wordsmith in me was working overtime again. My eye caught a framed piece of lined notebook paper on the wall. "Is that one of Paul's poems?"

"It is. Katherine and I took him to New Hampshire a couple of years ago. He wrote that looking out the window of the inn toward Mount Sunapee. Read it if you'd like."

In a clear voice, respecting each word, she read,

"'**September Sunset**

'When the autumn sun sets on the mountain,
Squeezing light to a golden tone,
Gilding houses, and barns, and meadows, and trees,
I revel at rosy cirrus clouds enfolding a hyacinth sky.
I wonder at Purple slopeside cleavages, shadowy and mysterious.

'On this late ninth month evening, summer's last robin skips
Over emerald blades of grass toward his mate, singing,
Fly with me to a warmer clime 'fore winter's chill descends.

'Dusk veils the scene and I mourn the loss of color, and of warmth,
Waning as the massive mountain yields to the starry night.

'Thanks for the trip, Paul.'"

"He called it his Whitmanesque response to the sunset," Max said.

"Delightful. And what's the medal hanging from the frame for?"

"It's a St. Nicholas medal. Paul gave it to me to keep me safe."

"Does it?"

"No, but whenever I see it I'm reminded of my little brother's absolute faith in me, and that gives me strength."

"Max, did you ever tell anyone about that day at the boxes?"

"Never. Did you?"

"No. Sometimes I wonder if it really happened."

"Oh, it happened. It's still happening."

"How do you mean?"

"I guess you should know. There's a reason I can't go to your apartment, or almost anywhere except here and my house, unless Katherine's with me. I have panic attacks and a condition called agoraphobia. I experience an unexplained dread in certain situations. I've had the problem for eight years now, and I've worked out ways to handle it, but the truth is, it's controlling my life."

"Is there a cure?"

"I'm working with a therapist who has a technique he calls 'Immunization.' It's like taking baby steps, facing each terror in a safe environment until I become immune to it. Can't say I see any change so far."

"So I guess you think your condition is a result of the violence of that day? Or maybe the violence you lived with every day. You know, Max, your father and my mother would be charged with child abuse today for the way they treated us."

"True, but life was so hard then, with the war and rationing. Kids were just another possession, or a burden. Didn't you think everybody lived the way we did then? I did."

"I did too, until I met Kate Larson's mother. Remember Kate? When we were in fifth grade she lived near Beech Street School. She used to take me home for lunch sometimes. The first time I went there, Mrs. Larson opened the door, smiled at me, and said, 'Hello, Susan. I'm so glad you're here.' I wanted her to adopt me. That's when I discovered kids could have a life much different from ours."

"Well, no one can pinpoint what started my problem, but the onset of my troubles suggests that day."

"Can I help?"

"Just telling you helps. I'm living with secrets at my job, with the family. I'm lying. I hate it. I'm not a liar. And I'm not a coward, but when an attack happens I have no control over my body. Katherine is my shield. She's a lifesaver."

Indispensable. "Well, you must have a class soon. I should go. I enjoyed this chat. Can we do it again?"

"Absolutely."

For the next week I spent hours canceling the lease, phone and utilities at my Chicago apartment, as well as having my mail forwarded. Rather than go back to pack my few things, I asked a good friend in my old building to stay with the movers while they packed in exchange for the sofa and upholstered chair she had always admired. I cooked meals for my dad, bought a wicker sofa and chair at the Salvation Army Store, and started to look for work. The closest publishing houses were in Boston so I answered a classified ad for a part time job at the *Oakhill Chronicle* doing local interest stories.

9

Commitment

At noon, a week after our lunch visit, Susan burst into my office shouting, "I saw him!"

"Hi Sue." Standing and snuffing out my cigarette, I asked, "Who'd you see that got you so excited? Paul Newman? Jack Kennedy?" Then I noticed how distressed she was. I took her hand and guided her to the overstuffed chair. "Here, have a seat. Take a deep breath and tell me what happened."

"Max," she said, grasping the arm of the chair. "I saw the man ... from the boxes."

Reaching up with my right thumb, I touched the scar under my chin. "That's impossible. According to the papers he didn't die in the fire, but he's long gone from here. Don't kid me like that."

Catching a deep breath, Susan exhaled, and said, "It's true. I would never kid you about that. And there's more ... he's my boss. I got a job at the paper," she stumbled on, "and an hour ago my editor gave me a tour of the building and introduced me to Henry Miller, the transition person from the New York company that bought the *Chronicle*. I didn't think I'd ever see him again ... but I just did. He's here. In Oakhill!" Her face paled.

"Okay," I said, as I walked to the water cooler in the corner. "Have a drink of water. Calm down and let's consider this. I expect being in that building again upset you."

Handing her the cup, I said, "First of all, why would the man come back here after committing a crime. That makes no sense."

Susan closed her eyes, sipped the water, and said, "Who knows that, Max?"

After another sip, and a deep breath, she said, "No one knows a crime was committed that day except you and I, Paul, and the man who did it. We know a bomb destroyed the factory, but the rest of the world believes it was a lightning strike. He worked there long enough to plan that senseless attack, and then we spoiled his plans."

She's right. My mind raced as I sat back down. Can't let her walk out of here believing she saw him. It couldn't be him. "How did he look?"

"Well, when I first met him I just had a feeling of déjà vu, like we'd met before, but I couldn't place him. His hair is grey at the temples, and he has glasses. When he stood I could see that he walks with a cane to support his left side. His face looks different from what I remember, of course my memory could be distorted. But then he spoke ... Max, I could never forget that voice."

Sitting up I blurted out, "Wait a minute. Did he recognize you?"

"Not at all. We never said our names that day, and I was nine years old with pigtails. He didn't pay much attention to me then anyway. Even if I acted surprised today, it would be normal for me to be nervous meeting the paper's new manager for the first time. Max, what should we do?"

"Nothing," I settled back in my chair. "He doesn't know who we are, and no one besides us kids knows we were at the factory that day. Susan, I realize this has upset you, but I can't accept that the person you met is the man. I can't believe he wouldn't high tail it back to Germany right after the war."

"Germany! What do you mean Germany? How would you know the man is German? Max, you know more about this than you're telling me."

"Yeah. Well, you know, I picked up his knife that day."

"No. I didn't know it. What else don't I know? What else are you keeping from me, Max?"

"Nothing else, Sue, honest. Well, I looked up the writing on the knife handle, and it's called a trench knife, issued to German Army soldiers. Now he could have found it in a shop somewhere. But I also learned that during the war America refitted existing factories to build weapons, and I believe that's what happened at the factory. It's not so hard to figure out that the bombing wasn't senseless, but sabotage."

Looking into her face, I tried to be convincing. "So you see, he wouldn't stay here after the war. He'd go home as fast as he could. It's weird that the *Chronicle* is in the same building, and that's the problem here, okay?"

"Wait a minute. If he's a German saboteur, then we need to call the FBI and expose him. He committed a war crime."

"Hold on. We committed a crime too. We broke into the factory. And besides an old German army knife, what do we have to back up a story that a crime happened at all? We were kids. That's pretty flimsy justification for going to the FBI."

My office wasn't built for pacing, but I had to get up and walk off the jitters flipping my belly.

"Look," I said, "we have daily, real life problems to deal with. It doesn't make sense to take huge risks to dig up something that happened twenty years ago. I'll find out who this Henry Miller is, and I promise I'll prove to you he's just a guy from New York trying to do his job."

"Maybe, but I'll never get that voice out of my head. I'm just as convinced as when I walked in here. It's him. I'm glad I don't have to go to the office. As I write each piece I can send in my stories. What about Paul? Should we tell him?"

"No. Paul's recovering from a bout of bronchitis. He needs rest now."

"Okay, I'll promise not to do anything about this if you'll promise we can talk as soon as you find out about Mr. Miller."

"Absolutely. Meanwhile give me a call whenever you want. Anytime at all. Are you okay to go home?"

"I'm fine," she said, though the furrows in her brow said something different. "See you later."

How can I research this guy? Who knows about everyone in this town? I picked up the phone. "Hello, Maria? It's Max."

"Hi, little brother. Need a haircut?"

"No, but I do have a favor to ask."

"Anything, sure."

"Well, I'd like to find out about the new Managing Editor at the *Chronicle*. His name's Henry Miller."

"Oh, I know him. He's in the Chamber. I met him at the Annual Dinner. Seemed nice. What do you want to know?"

"Things like where he moved from, the name of his paper in New York, anything personal really. But please keep it between us. Is Mrs. Berkeley still your client?"

"Every Friday at nine. She'll be here in the morning. I'll do what I can, discreetly. Do I get to find out why?"

"Not yet. Right now let's just say I'm curious."

"That's a deal. Take care. Bye."

The next morning Maria called to say the name of Henry Miller's parent paper was the *New York City News*, and he commuted from his house in Beechwood on Long Island, New York, where his wife and son lived.

It wasn't much, but enough so I could explore the facts a bit more. I had to get to the Boston Public Library and use their microfiche files. The easiest way would be to take the train to Boston, then the subway to Copley Square. But trains are confining and crowded. I couldn't. I asked Katherine to drive all the way on Route 28. We went through the small towns, and it took twice as long, but I couldn't let fear control every aspect of my life. I had to accomplish my tasks in spite of my problems, and with Katherine's help I could.

I found no newspaper in the microfiche files for Beechwood, Long Island, New York, but I discovered it's located in Yarmouth County, and the library had files for the *Yarmouth County Courant* since before the war. I pored through. Americans of German ancestry heavily populated the whole county. Many articles before the war were devoted to the activities of a German/American youth camp in the town of Yarmouth called Camp Klein. Several were written by angry citizens who condemned the activities there as un-American. One article concerned vandalism at the camp by local teenagers protesting the Sunday parades of campers, marching down Main Street and to the beach. I found a shocking photo of a campers' parade with the American Flag and the Swastika side by side. Another portrayed hundreds of campers raising their arms in the *Heil Hitler* salute. This was in America, in NewYork. I had no idea that kind of thing happened here on such a scale before the war.

The third photo took my breath away. I looked directly into the smiling face of the man. Five Camp Klein boys were about to embark on the SS *Europa* for a trip they had won to Germany. The name of the boy with the familiar face was Heinrich Mueller.

That's too easy. The boys were all residents of Beechwood. I asked the librarian to copy the photo and left with the ominous knowledge that Susan's intuition had been right.

Now I needed to determine what would make Miller come back to Oakhill. He had created a successful career after the incident. Why risk his success, his family's happiness, and his freedom by coming back here? Could his need for revenge be so great?

That was hard to believe, but if it was the case, then Susan, Paul, and I were in serious danger. *He's a trained killer. If he finds us, he won't spare our lives again*. I decided to give myself time before telling Susan. She'd want to call the FBI right away. Maybe I could make Miller aware of the threat to himself by staying here. If I could intimidate him into leaving town we could avoid any trouble. I typed up some notes on the typewriter in my office, and mailed them to Miller, one a day for three days.

I wrote:

I KNOW WHO YOU ARE!
I KNOW WHAT YOU DID AUGUST 16TH, 1943.
LEAVE OAKHILL BY JUNE 8TH OR I GO TO THE FBI

I waited until the next Friday, June 9th, to call the *Chronicle* office asking for Mr. Miller. When Miller answered the phone in his velvety voice, a chill went through my body. I regressed to the child in the boxes. I said, "Wrong number." and hung up. I'd been foolish.

I could not play with Susan and Paul's lives like this. "Get hold of yourself, Mr. Ski."

I called Susan, "Can you come to my office?"

"Be there in five minutes."

Just before she opened the door, my phone rang. Paul said, "Max, something strange just happened. I received an envelope in my Post Office box addressed to me with no sender's name or return address. The clerk must have written in the box number because it's in pencil. The notes say something about August 16th. I'm sure they're intended for someone else, but I don't like it. Feels creepy."

"I don't think it'll happen again. Just some kids pulling pranks at the end of the school year. Tomorrow's Saturday. Katherine and I will come out to the cabin if you're planning to be home."

"Thanks. That'd be great. I'll make lunch. See you about noon."

I looked at Susan sitting in the overstuffed chair, and said, "I've made things worse."

"Tell me, Max."

"First, I'm sorry I doubted you. You're right. Henry Miller is Heinrich Mueller, the German saboteur."

"Much as I like being right, I hoped this time I'd be wrong."

"I found this photo of him as a teenager," I said, showing her the clipping. "There's no question it's the man. Now he has a name, two in fact. The big question is why would he come back here? He's successful, with a family and a home in New York. Why risk all that?"

Susan leaned forward toward the desk. "He's not risking anything at all by being here, Max. He's in the clear. There's no question about his being there the day of the fire. According to the Oakhill Fire and Police Departments he was the victim of a lightning strike, seriously injured in the accident. Our interference nearly cost him his life, and left him crippled. I think he's here for revenge, to find us and torture us as much as he's been tortured."

"I need to tell you something else. I did something I regret."

The pain in my eyes must have touched Susan's heart because she looked at me with such sympathy. She's the only person on earth I can talk to about what I've done. I'm so glad she's here.

"What did you do that makes you feel so bad?"

"Well, when I discovered his real identity, I tried to scare Miller away. I sent him some notes, telling him I know what he did and he'd better leave town. It seems he thinks Paul sent them because he forwarded them to him. That's what the call was about when you came in. Susan, I've put my little brother in harm's way."

"Okay. We need to visit Paul and tell him what we know. At least then he'll be warned."

"Paul doesn't remember the boxes," I said.

"Of course he does. He was six. I remember things when I was six, and this is not something he'd be likely to forget."

"You don't understand, Sue. There's something more you need to know. See, about five years ago, a neighbor found Paul wandering around Oakhill Cente in what the doctors call a 'fugue' state. He didn't recognize the neighbor, and in fact he had no personal memories whatsoever, like his name, where he lived, or us. Instead of bringing him home, the local cops, who all know him, brought him to St. Michael's and called my mom. He didn't even know her."

Susan bit her lip but didn't speak.

"They did all kinds of medical tests and found nothing physically wrong with him. The doctors said the repeated adrenalin overload of witnessing acts of violence causes the brain to defend itself. It shuts down the area holding not only those memories, but also most others. The name for it is psychogenic amnesia."

"You're saying he still hasn't recovered his memory?"

"I am. He spent six months in rehab. We brought him old photos and his books, whatever we could think of to help him remember. A breakthrough happened the day before Thanksgiving. We brought him his favorite mince pie. He didn't even realize he said it, but the aroma of the hot pie triggered something, because he said, 'Hey, smells like Thanksgiving in here!'

"Mom and I had a hard time not to cry. He just ate his pie, but the incident made us believe there could be some improvement. His therapists encouraged us to think of other smells he might recognize, like flowers or other foods. The recognition hasn't happened again, yet.

"Mom visited every day at the rehab. When she told him she was his mother, he said, 'When I look at you, I see me. Hi Mom!' She really did cry that day.

"Sometimes I wonder if he remembers anything, or if he just accepts what we've told him about his life. I believe he knows we love him. When I told him about the time he gave me the St. Nicholas medal his eyes filled up, and he said he hoped it kept me safe. I want to believe he remembers me.

"Today I decided to wear the medal always, to remind me not to let my little brother down, particularly after what I just did. It's my responsibility to protect him. In rehab, part of his treatment was to keep a journal. Instead he wrote poetry. The collection became *Echoes*."

"Wow," Susan said. "That's a lot to take in. Now I understand why Christine suggested I wait for you to visit him. Should I go?"

"Yes. Come with me tomorrow. We'll tell him who you are. Of course, we won't mention anything about that day. In fact, if you don't mind, will you drive me? I'll give Katherine some time off."

"I'll pick you up just before noon."

As Susan got up to leave, I handed her a book. "I think you should read this before seeing Paul." I gave her my well-worn copy of *Echoes*.

She'd only need to glance through the Table of Contents to see that Paul wrote in a variety of forms, but what astounded me most when I first read it were some of the titles, "The Ballad of the Black Knight," "King's Castle," then "Ode to Fire," and "Rain."

She'll see The Black Knight in the ballad is Henry Miller. It's the story of how the knight finessed his way into the castle, promising exotic spices from the East.

Then, when he entered the king's chamber, he turned into a fire-breathing black dragon with red tipped wings and knife-like claws. He slashed the king with "curling saber claws" releasing a "flood of royal crimson blood." Paul has no memory of it, but I remember that August 16th well, and have the scar to prove it happened.

Many of the subjects for Paul's poems were from our playtime at the boxes, like a sonnet in perfect Shakespearean form titled "Pirates."At least four poems referred to the day of the fire.

What if Henry Miller has seen the book?

I hadn't considered that disturbing possibility before.

As soon as I got into the car on Saturday, Susan said, "I read *Echoes*, and I don't understand."

"Okay, he does not consciously remember any of his young childhood. I believe that. But, in some area of his brain, experiences linger and he expresses them as poetry. It's a bit like a person who has a stroke and can't speak, but he can sing a Christmas carol word for word. It's different parts of a person's brain operating beyond their control."

"But this is dangerous, Max. If Henry Miller reads the book he'll think Paul remembers everything."

"I thought of that yesterday. Look, let's take things one step at a time. Maybe we can reason with Miller. We're all adults now. What can he do to us anyway? What he did seems terrible to us, but in his mind he was just doing his duty. And he certainly has paid a price. I'm still not convinced what his real reason is for coming back,"

Paul had built his cabin halfway down the steep incline from the road to the pond, affording him a breathtaking water view. As we were snaking our way down on the curved driveway Susan said, “We need the FBI. We need to expose him and get him deported back to Germany.”

I knocked. “Hi Paul.” Then I entered the cabin’s living room. Paul sat in his recliner with the phone in his hand making that sound it does when it’s off the hook. “Max. You’re here,” he said in a whisper.

“What is it, Paul? You’re shaking. What happened?”

The blood had drained from his face. Even his lips were white.

“I got a strange phone call. Scared me a bit. A man called and said he was The Black Knight. That’s a character in a poem I wrote. There’s no such person really,” Paul said quietly.

“What else did he say?” I replaced the receiver and knelt closer so I could hear him

Gathering enough breath to speak, Paul stared at the floor. “He said he would come back to storm the castle again ... and this time no one would escape. ‘Be prepared for the worst,’ he said. Then he said I’d better tell the king.” Looking up at me, he said, “Max, I don’t understand. Did I do something bad before I can remember? Something that would make a person this angry with me?”

My chest tightened, and I had a lump in my throat. He was innocent, unable to understand why a vengeful bully would threaten him. He became a victim only because he was there, in the boxes, playing a game with his big brother. It was my fault he was suffering. I had to fix this, I had to make this anguish in my brother's face go away. A flash of anger shot through my body. I felt the heat of it in my face. Saboteur or not, I'd stop him, dead, in his tracks.

I closed my eyes, exhaled, and focused on concealing my outrage from Paul. "No." I said, as I put my hand on his arm. "You've never done anything bad in your life. This is a nutty person trying to scare you. How about coming to stay with me and Katherine for a while, until he finds someone else to bother. You may be more comfortable than being out here on your own."

I looked up at Susan. Her hand covered her mouth to stifle a gasp at hearing Paul's phone conversation. Whispering between clenched teeth, I said, "Let's get him."

10

Good Day/Bad Day

Susan had to admire Paul's courage when he refused Max's invitation to stay with him and Katherine. As much as Max made a logical case for Paul to visit with them, he said, "This is my home. If I haven't wronged anyone there's no reason for me to leave it."

"Okay then, what if I stay here with you for a couple of days?"

Susan glanced at Max and raised her eyebrows as if to say, and how will you do that with your problem?

"Thanks, Max. You're always welcome here, but it's really not necessary. I overreacted." The color had returned to his cheeks. He grinned up at Susan. "So, who's this young lady you've brought to visit me?"

"This is Susan," Max said. "She lived next door to us when we were kids. She played with the twins and you and me. We went to the Saturday movies a lot, and played marbles and fifty scatter. We were the neighborhood gang when you were six."

"Hello, Susan. Please don't be offended that I didn't recall. I have a memory problem, but I'm sure it'll come back to me. Sounds like we had fun."

"We did. That time seemed like one long happy summer." Sitting on the couch across from Paul, Susan noticed the latest issue of the *Chronicle* on the pine coffee table between them. On the front page was a photo of Paul outside the cabin. *There's proof Miller knows not only who Paul is, but also where he lives.*

Picking up the paper and showing it to Max, she said, "Congratulations on your award. I understand your book is a big hit with the teenagers. For the first time in generations, kids are reading poetry."

"Yeah. Never expected that response. Maybe it's because I'm not much older than them. It's a puzzle, but a pleasant one. Ready for lunch?"

The warm yeasty smell of newly baked bread lured Susan into the kitchen. Open shelves displayed colorful dishes and glassware, as well as packages of dried fruits, grains, beans, and staples for baking. A counter crafted from a wide oak board finished in a soft luster, separated the cooking from the dining area. It housed a gas stove with a deep green tile surround. They sat at an oval maple table in front of a large window with herbs growing in pots on the sill, overlooking the pond.

"I can see you like to cook," Susan said to Paul.

"I do. Next time I'll write a cookbook."

He served delicious chicken salad sandwiches with diced green grapes and chopped walnuts, on homemade bread, and oatmeal cookies for dessert.

After lunch, Max asked to see the envelope Paul had received. His notes were inside. He showed it to Susan. He was right. This was a reckless thing to do. I guess he tried to do the safe thing to protect himself from having to challenge Miller. Well, no more. After what Miller did to Paul today, Max will see this through. I wish we had a plan, though.

"So, what do you think?" Paul asked.

"I think it's the same nut who called you today," Max said. "We'll get to the bottom of this."

After lunch they took a walk down the steep path to the edge of Craggy Pond. Max told Susan he decided he would stay with Paul for a couple of days.

"Can you manage that?"

"I'm sure he has a small paper bag I can breathe into if I have to. I'll warn him about what may happen, but after seeing the newspaper, I can't leave him alone,"

An hour later Susan said goodbye to Paul, with thanks and a promise to meet again soon. Max walked her to the car.

"I'll have Katherine bring some clothes. It'll only be two nights. He'll go to New York Monday to do the *Today Show* on Tuesday morning. Meanwhile, let's consider our options. Make a list of things we can do. I'll call you tomorrow."

"Please be careful. We don't know for sure what this guy is capable of. One good thing, he'd have a hard time driving down this hill without being seen from the cabin."

"Don't worry. I was a kid the last time we met, but I could take him easily now. Let's both come up with some ideas. I'll talk to you tomorrow."

Sitting at her kitchen table, Susan wrote her list of evidence: Max had the knife and the scar from it, they knew Miller's real name, and they had a photo of him the way they remembered him. But the man was a killer. She and Max had no more expertise in that arena than they had as children eighteen years ago, and Miller knew about *Echoes* without knowing Paul doesn't really remember. "We have to call the FBI."

Max surprised her by agreeing when they talked the next day. "I don't want to do anything else to make things worse," he said. "I still have a week of school. Can you come to my office on Monday around ten? We'll call together."

They made an appointment with FBI Agent Tom Hanson for Tuesday afternoon.

Garroway saved Paul's interview until the end of his program on Tuesday morning, but Susan didn't mind watching the entertaining hour. His easy-going style made his guests and those watching feel as though he was speaking only to them. He introduced Paul in his smooth, resonant voice. "I hear you're quite a hit with the young folks. I'm always happy to hear people are reading."

"Thanks, I'm pleasantly surprised too," Paul said.

"Now, tell me, Paul. How do you come up with such a variety of ideas for your poems?"

"They come to me as impressions that I can't resist writing down."

"And you write them down with such vividness and energy, and in such a variety of forms."

"Yes, the subject of the poem usually dictates the form, but sometimes I mix them up deliberately, like a sonnet about pirates. Such a structured form about wild, undisciplined characters amuses me."

"In your 'Ode to Fire' I could feel the heat, taste the smoke, and see the flames. I guess the best compliment for any writer is for a reader to feel as if he's actually in the story world, and I can say that about several of your poems. I'm charmed and entertained by *Echoes*. Can't wait for your next work. Thanks for coming by, Paul." With his signature broad smile, Garroway looked directly into the camera. "That's it for today, folks." He held up his right hand, palm open, smiled, and said, "Peace."

Great job. He'll be happy with his day on national TV.

Henry liked to watch the *Today Show* while he dressed for work. That Garroway really knows how to handle people. As he turned the dial, someone was talking about pirates. "Oh, right, this is the day the brat's on TV. He's getting famous, and rich, because of me!"

When he was shaving Henry pressed too hard with the razor and cut his chin. He reached for his cane and knocked it off the edge of the sink onto the floor. "Everything's going wrong today!" He continued muttering as he finished his morning routine.

11

Reinforcements

The only comfortable place Susan and Max could talk freely with FBI Agent Tom Hanson was at Susan's apartment. She picked him up, and for the first time since Max's marriage he visited an unfamiliar place without Katherine. Agent Hanson drove up in a sleek black '61 Dodge Dart, wearing a dark blue suit and Aviator sunglasses. Tall and well-groomed, he walked with the confidence of a man who's in charge of things.

"Welcome, Agent Hanson," Susan said.

"Thanks. It might be easier for us to be on a first name basis. You can call me Tom." Then he asked Max and Susan about their current lives. Max told him about being an American history teacher, and married to Katherine. Susan admitted she aspired to be a writer, she was recently divorced, and currently doing local interest stories for the *Chronicle*.

When he asked why they called him, Max related the story of that August day at the boxes in detail. Then he told about Miller coming back to Oakhill, and the mixed-up attempt to intimidate him. Tom shook his head. "I believe you're telling the truth, but just because something really happened doesn't mean the story's believable, especially to a judge. First he'll want hard evidence that a crime had been committed. Then we have to prove that Miller perpetrated that crime. So far there's not even evidence of a crime.

"Also, the case is eighteen years old. There's no time limit on sabotage cases, but there's no fresh evidence either. The best piece you have is his real name. We have rooms full of data on people who were sympathetic to the German cause during World War Two. Let me see what the name turns up. Meanwhile, don't do anything else like writing notes. I'd try to stay with Paul if you can. It seems Miller doesn't know yet that you two were there. If anyone is in danger, he is." He gave Susan his card, said he'd get back to them soon, and asked, "What was the name of the factory?"

"Sam Wilson Manufacturing, though we don't know what they made there," Susan said. "We just called it the factory."

"It's at 652 Main Street, right? I'll see what I can find." And he left.

"I feel better knowing we've got Tom," Max said. "He evens the playing field."

"And you're feeling okay?"

"Yeah, no problem. Maybe I'm starting my immune therapy on my own. Or maybe my concern for Paul's safety overrides any concerns I have about myself. If you'll take me back to school, I'll pick up some finals to correct, and then I'll get some clothes and go back to Paul's. He'll be home around six from New York."

"I'll drive you."

When Susan and Max arrived at Paul's a little after six his car was in the drive. The front door of the cabin was open. "He must have just gotten in," Max said as he entered the living room. "Oh my God."

Susan followed him in. "Oh, no!"

Magazines and books were scattered about the room, tables were overturned and their lamps flung to the floor.

"Paul?" Max called.

"In here."

The kitchen looked like a war zone. Sacks of flour, beans, and sugar were ripped open and their contents strewn around the room. Opened jars of spices, slashed boxes of pastas, and sliced packets of dried fruit were scattered across the counter and the floor. A haze of flour had settled on every surface. Paul sat in the one upright chair, staring at the empty spice jar in his hand, as if it were not real. On top of the mess on the table lay a black feather, probably from a crow, with fire engine red nail polish painting the tip.

"It was him," Paul said, his voice barely audible. "The Black Dragon. Why would anyone do such a thing, Max?"

"We'll fix it, Paul," Max said, squeezing Paul's arm to reassure him. He slipped the feather into his pocket, picked up the receiver of the wall phone, and called Tom Hanson.

"It looks like someone wanted to go wild and make a huge mess. The jimmy marks on the back door are the only real damage I can see." Then he told Tom about the feather and its significance.

"Call the police," Tom said, "and make a report. I'll call Chief Engels now to let him know I'm involved and to keep it quiet. Henry, or someone he hired, committed a crime, but we don't want to arrest him just for breaking and entering. It'd be best to get Paul out of there as soon as he talks to the police. Keep in touch, okay?"

"Right, I'll take Paul home with me."

"You realize, this is just a teaser," Tom said. "I'll call you as soon as I know more."

"Thanks, Tom," Max said, and dialed the police.

Susan tried to distract Paul. "I saw the TV show, Paul. You were terrific."

"Thanks. I totally relaxed. So different from the *Chronicle* reporter who insisted that *Echoes* represented real memories. Garroway listened and cared about my answers."

"Paul," Max said, "this time I hope you agree that you'll need to come home with me while a cleaning crew comes into the house."

"Absolutely. Thanks."

To Susan, Max said, "I'll have to keep coming up with new excuses for him to stay there when that one wears out."

···❖···

Two weeks went by before Susan heard from Tom Hanson. She wrote an article about the local Garden Club planting perennials at the Oakhill Free Library, and interviewed watercolor artists at the opening of their show at the Center Gallery. She attended and wrote a review of the new play at the Opera House, an original drama called *A Likely Story* about a heist at a library. The play concerned two cleaning people working at a mansion who accidentally included a first edition of *Alice in Wonderland* with the books that were donated to the library's annual book sale, and their bumbling attempts to get it back.

Tom's words that Miller didn't yet know she and Max were in the factory resonated in her mind. She wanted to avoid making a mistake that might let him find out. Mailing her articles to Mr. Cain, the editor who had hired her at the paper, allowed her to submit her work comfortably.

She had dinner with her dad twice each week. They talked about his fishing friends and his childhood on a farm in Maine. They avoided talking about her mom. Susan wanted to catch up on each other's lives without that heavy distraction.

But as they sat over coffee the last time they had dinner, her dad said, "I know you and your mom had a rough go of it."

Susan raised her hand to dispel the notion, but he continued, "No, it's true. She was an angry woman. Her obsession with keeping the house spotless caused problems between us too, like when I'd leave the newspaper on the chair in the living room. I often felt her reaction was overly dramatic, that something else was the real cause of her being so cross with me. I never did figure it out.

"But I wondered if she was resentful of our middle class life. I sensed she felt she was entitled to something better. I know she yelled at you, and not in pleasant terms."

"Yeah, her favorite word was 'stupid.' She didn't call me stupid, just said things like, 'that was a stupid thing to do.' It felt the same.

"Dad, you might as well know, she not only yelled, she hit me, every day. Starting with the comb when she braided my hair in the morning. Our house was safe for me only when you were home. I can tell you this now because I've gotten over it ... doesn't impact me anymore."

"Oh, honey. I didn't know what was happening to you. But, I should have known. I should have protected you. I didn't do my job. I'm so sorry I didn't."

Those words broke her mother's hold on her. In a flash she realized the problem was her mother, not her. Hearing that he, too, was a victim of her mother's rage meant it wasn't her fault, none of it, nor were her mother's cruel words the truth. To hear him say he was sorry for not protecting her unleashed a flood of grateful tears. Right there in the Oakhill Diner, Susan went around to his side of the table, sobbed, and hugged her dad hard. They sat for a while, her head on his shoulder, his arm around hers.

Susan called Max when she got home. "Hi. Tom called and asked if we could meet at my place tomorrow at two."

"Sure. School's out so I have free time. I'll drive over."

"Are you sure?"

"No, but I'll give it a shot. If I have to turn around, I'll call you. Is that okay?"

"You bet."

Max left his house the next day with Katherine and Paul cooking a gourmet dinner. He arrived early at Susan's. The conversation she'd had with her father was still on her mind. "Max, I had a talk with my dad last night. It changed the way I see my mother's behavior."

"No kidding. So, have you forgiven her?"

"No. That's the point. I don't think forgiveness is needed. My dad told me he was as confused by her violent outbursts at him, as I was when she did it to me. So, you see, all this time I believed I was to blame for her anger, but I wasn't. The problem was hers, not mine. It's just who she was."

"I think I understand," Max said. "I needed distance from my dad to get a different angle on the way he treated me too. His behavior is still not forgivable, but now I can understand his intentions. I've made my peace with it."

"Dad also apologized for not protecting me," Susan said, "and those words filled a gap, strengthened our bond. If I was a disappointment to my mom, then she didn't know me. I don't think she ever bothered to know me."

"And that was her loss, my girl."

Susan passed out the iced teas she had prepared when Tom arrived. "Thanks. Well, I discovered Sam

Wilson Manufacturing was an assembly line operation making thousands of components for telephones. Then, when Northern Electric landed a military contract for radar and sonar devices, they approached Wilson with an offer to retrofit his factory and make the equipment. He changed from an assembly line to a job-shop process, educated the mechanics, and filled the contracts. So, they were making highly specialized war materials when the factory was destroyed. That's a strong case for sabotage."

Susan and Max glanced at each other, knowing for sure they had been involved in a war crime.

"I didn't have as much luck researching Heinrich Mueller," Tom said. "I called Beechwood and talked to his mother as an old friend trying to locate him. Her name is Trudy. She owns an interior design business called Roomscapes in the center of town.

"Everything fits until he graduated from high school, but then he vanished from the files until he returned to Beechwood five years later as Henry Miller."

"He must have returned to Germany to become a saboteur during those five years," Susan said.

"According to his mother, after high school he worked at Ford Motor Company in Dearborn, Michigan, and served in the US Army. There are no records to support either of those claims. I have an idea where he might have been for those years after high school, and you may be close to the truth, Susan, but if my hunch is right we'll never get records.

"Your description of his behavior when he found you in the factory, that he engaged you and tried to gain your trust, makes me think he might have been trained at the Brandenburg Sabotage School. Deception and finesse were fundamental there. It was the only one of its kind in Germany, but we weren't able to get much in the way of documents at the end of the war. I'll keep looking. How's Paul doing?"

"Really well," Max said. "He's teaching Katherine some of his recipes, and we're going to look for a dog for him. A German shepherd should be the right breed. I keep delaying the cleaning company's final run-through at his house to keep him with me longer. I'll see his doctor at St. Michael's Rehab next week for advice on the best way to handle negative information, but I won't offer any details. This is heavy stuff for a fragile person to handle. Maybe it would be better if Paul never knows."

"You're quiet, Susan," Tom said. "What's on your mind?"

"I'm worried about Paul. The level of Miller's violence has intensified. We won't mention the notes, but first he made the threatening phone call, then he trashed Paul's house, and he thinks he's getting away with it. What's next?"

"That kind of acceleration is typical criminal behavior," Tom said, "which is why we want to get as much on him as quickly as we can. In fact, Susan, your job at the paper can be an advantage to us before Miller knows you were involved, if you're willing."

"Of course. I'll do whatever I can."

"Can you get us into the building after hours when Miller's not there?"

"Yes. I'm working independently and don't keep regular hours. Mr. Cain gave me a key to open both exterior doors. I also have the Press Card with my name and photo on it. I could pretend I forgot something when the printers are there, or later when the paper's being packed for distribution. Those people have never seen me, in fact I haven't been back to the building since the day I met Miller."

"Good," Tom got up to leave. "We can install a wiretap on his phone and maybe discover some of his plans. I'll call to make a time. Don't despair, we'll stay on top of this. Keep in touch."

As soon as Tom left, Susan asked, "So, how was the drive?"

"Fine. You know, Katherine and I have been so careful these past years to avoid my triggers that I haven't had an attack for quite a while. Maybe it's not because I'm being careful. Maybe I'm better."

"Well, let's not start looking for a bridge to cross, but maybe the therapist is right. This small step made you more confident. I'm happy to hear it."

That evening, Michael Hathaway called Susan. He was editor of the Oakhill High School Newspaper when they were in school. "Hi Susan, I saw you at the reunion but didn't get a chance to say hello."

"Hi Michael. Good to hear from you. Wasn't the reunion fun?"

"It was. The thing our high school class took most seriously was having a good time. We had four years of fun. I'm calling because I just came by some tickets for Sunday's matinee of *Camelot.* It's at the Schubert with Julie Andrews and Richard Burton, and I wondered if you'd like to go."

"I would love that. I have the record of *Camelot.* I think I know every word. And we can catch up on the past ten years."

"Great. I'll pick you up at one o'clock. The matinee's at two. I live here in Boston, so I'll cook us an early dinner, if that's okay, and I'll have you home before eight."

"Sounds great, Michael. See you Sunday. Bye"

I have a date ... with a smart, handsome confident man. She started humming, "Camelot, dada, dada, dadadada."

12

Scene of the Crime

"Let's go in Saturday night," Tom said when he called the next day. "The *Chronicle* doesn't have a Sunday edition, so no workers should be in the building around midnight, but we can still be prepared to use your excuse if someone is. Ready?"

"I am," Susan replied.

"I'll pick you up about 11:30. Wear dark clothes and your Press Card."

Tom parked in the truck yard behind the building. A twinge in her belly as she opened the car door reminded Susan of her mission here. No one in sight, and just a sliver of moon. She thought about the many other times she broke into this building when she was nine years old, though it didn't seem like breaking in then.

They climbed the stairs to the exterior door. Tom used Susan's key, and they entered the room she remembered as the boxes. She took a deep breath and smiled at Tom who looked down as if to say, "You okay?"

She nodded and they proceeded through the corridor to Henry's office. Tom ran his fingers around the wood frame to checked for an alarm, then he easily picked the lock on the office door. It took only seconds for him to take the phone receiver apart and install the bug. He had made arrangements for the recording equipment to be stashed in an old car parked at the gas station next door.

A noise!

Susan looked up at Tom questioning with her expression,'What do we do now?'

Women's voices shattered the silence, and office lights wiped out the cover of darkness. Creaky cart wheels rolled down the aisle of the office toward them. Cleaning people. Susan's heart quickened. She held her breath. They crouched behind Henry's desk.

"Go into the ladies' room," Tom said. "You'll have to use your Press Card to distract them. I'll slide out the back. You go to the front door and I'll meet you outside."

Susan nodded yes, hoping she could pull it off. She went into the ladies' room, turned on the light and started to wash her hands when the door opened.

"Oh," one woman said. "We didn't expect anyone to be here."

"Hi. I work here and had to get some notes from my desk. Here's my ID. See, I'm not a burglar." They laughed.

Looking at the press card, one of them said, "I know that name. You're the lady who wrote the review of *A Likely Story*. I thought your article was funnier than the play."

"Thanks. It was a catchy play, had lots of twists and turns. I hear it had a good run."

"Well I saw it," the woman replied, "and I think your article was funnier. You should write a play, a funny one."

"Maybe someday I will. Well, I'm off. Nice to meet you."

"You too," they said.

Susan walked, barely resisting the urge to run, to the front door and Tom's waiting car.

"Are you okay?" he asked.

"Yeah," Susan replied, taking a deep breath as she closed the car door. "Better than okay. I feel energized, more alive right now than I've felt in a long time."

"A close encounter does get the heart pounding," he said.

Tom drove into the gas station and checked something in the glove compartment of the old car parked there. "The bug's working fine," he said. They started up Main Street again.

"Y'know, Tom, I didn't realize how much of a burden keeping the secret of the factory explosion was until I said it out loud. It's empowering to get it out in the open."

"Glad I can help. I talked about your case with an agent in our office. She works with kids who've witnessed a crime. She said witnessing violence carries as much trauma as being the victim. It's a delicate dance to give children permission to speak while being sure they don't feel threatened or guilty. Seems kids see themselves as victims until they're allowed to tell the secret, even into adulthood. Makes me happy to hear you're relieved of that burden. It's mine now.

"Say, if you're not tired, how about going to the diner for coffee? It's the only place open all night in Oakhill."

"Great. I know I couldn't sleep for a while after our escapade."

The diner was a beacon of light in the middle of darkened Oakhill center. Its aluminum façade gleamed under a streetlight, and red neon hollered "Oakhill Diner" from its roof. A warm glow of lights from the rectangular windows enticed Susan and Tom inside. Red vinyl upholstered the booths and covered the round barstool seats perched on silver pedestals at the counter. The jukebox blared the latest Chuck Berry tune.

A couple in the last booth leaned across the table so they could hear each other, and three men at the counter laughed and bragged about their bowling scores. It could have been noon on a Saturday inside the diner. Susan and Tom chose a booth near the door, and ordered coffees. Sitting forward, arms on the table, Susan said, "I'm curious. What made you want to be an FBI agent?"

"Well, I grew up in a city with a significant mafia presence. My dad had his own business refinishing high-end furniture pieces for the local interior design companies. He was an artist. A stubborn one. He wouldn't cooperate when the local hoodlums contacted him for a piece of his pie for insurance.

"So, I watched his business, and then his health, deteriorate. None of the local designers resisted the mob's suggestion that they avoid my dad. When I decided to get into law enforcement I chose to be an agent at the Federal Bureau. This is my way of saying 'Stop' to the criminals who broke my dad's spirit."

"I'm glad one of us is following the right path."

"You will be too. Be patient. You'll be an author one day soon."

"Hope so. Wow, it's after one o'clock. I think I can sleep now. Thanks for the coffee and conversation," Susan said.

If there could be a perfect date, Sunday would qualify. Heading toward Boston, Michael said, "I'm so glad I caught up with you. I was on the committee for the reunion, so I was running around with a few duties to do, and then you were gone."

"I'm glad too. You're right about our class having fun. Remember when we used to go to Joyce Kimball's house after school, roll up the living room rug, and dance until her mom was due to come home from work?"

"Yeah, remember the time we got caught?"

" ... and Mrs. Kimball joined right in."

For the rest of the ride they talked about some of the silly happenings at Oakhill High, particularly at the school paper.

From the moment the curtain opened, *Camelot* was spectacular. Susan was enthralled, not only with the set and glorious music but also with the tragic love story of Arthur, Guinevere and Lancelot, in that perfect place where it's only allowed to rain after sundown.

For the first time experiencing the story she knew so well, she noticed how Arthur changed from being "scared!" as he hid in the forest, to ultimately becoming a wise and noble king, worthy of legend. As he matured she championed his courageous determination to establish a land where justice triumphs over evil. She was grateful the exit music took several minutes, long enough to dry her eyes before the house lights came on.

On the way to Michael's condo in the Back Bay neighborhood of the city, he asked, "So, what have you been up to since high school?'

"Oh, I was an English major at UMass, still thinking I'd be a writer some day. Then I married and moved to Chicago, but we recently divorced. I decided to come back to be with my dad when mom died."

"Sorry, I didn't know you'd lost your mom recently."

"Thanks. Now I'm doing local interest stories for the *Chronicle*."

"Great! So you are a writer."

"Yeah ... I guess I am."

Michael owned an elegant, simply furnished condo on Marlboro Street. For dinner he made a lasagne with crusty bread, a salad with raspberries, and Chianti to top it off.

"I didn't make dessert," he said.

"Oh, I don't need it," Susan replied. "That was a lovely dinner."

"No, I mean I didn't make it, but I picked up some cannolis in the North End this morning. Vanilla or chocolate?"

"Oh, chocolate, please. Nothing says dessert like chocolate. This day has been so much fun, Michael. I'm glad you called. And you're such a good cook."

"Comes with being a bachelor. If I want to eat, and that's one of my favorite activities, I had to learn. Now it's kind of a hobby."

After dessert and coffee they walked to Michael's car at the back of his building. As he held the door for her to get in, he said, "I'd like to have more days like this one."

They listened to radio music on the way home, comfortable with not talking.

At her door, Susan said, "It's early, but I feel a bit tired. Thanks for a wonderful day."

"I hope we can do this again."

"I'd like that," She stood on tiptoes to give him a kiss on the cheek.

"I'll call you soon," Michael said.

Susan got into her jammies, settled down with Channel Two's *Suspense Theatre*, and daydreamed of that chocolate cannoli. Wow, this day rates a ten.

Michael called several times in the next few weeks, each time enjoying long, getting-to-know-you-again conversations. On a sunny Sunday afternoon he invited Susan to picnic at Boston's Public Garden. They sat on a grassy knoll under the trees near Beacon Street to share the tuna salad sandwiches he'd made, then strolled to the suspension bridge to watch children and their parents on the swan boats. Weeping willows dotted the pond, dripping their feathery branches to sip from the water's edge. "Oh, look Michael," Susan said, grabbing his arm, as two live adult swans glided under the bridge just below them.

They strolled along winding paths lined with ribbons of red, pink, and yellow roses that exploded into gardens. Rounding a corner, they encountered lovers sharing a kiss. Susan grinned up a Michael, welcoming his lips, soft and sweet, on hers.

13

Agent Tom Hanson

I poked into the glove compartment of the old car parked at the gas station. *C'mon Henry, make a mistake.* He'd made lots of calls to his mother and wife in Beechwood, and to *NY City News*. Well, this is interesting. I wonder what he wants with the Mass. Department of Education.

"Yes, this is Henry Miller, Oakhill School Board. I'd like to inform the Department of our receipt of the standardized tests for next year. We'll be in touch as soon as the tests are administered and the data are calculated." Nothing incriminating here.

"Thanks for letting me leave this piece of junk here," I said to the gas station owner.

"For fifty bucks a month you can leave it there forever."

Back at the office in Boston I asked Larry, "Know anything about the Brandenburg Commandoes during the Second World War?"

"Only what's common knowledge. But there's a guy who writes articles in the Historical News section for the *German Journal* at Fort Myers in Florida. The magazine's written for the thousands of German immigrants down there. It has all kinds of news about events, films, restaurants, whatever. His expertise is German U-boats, but he may know something about Brandenburg."

"You are an encyclopedia, Larry. Thank you. I remember a case involving saboteurs in DC who came here on a German sub during the war. I think they were court-martialed and most were executed, quickly and quietly. Mostly I hope this guy'll know something about the Brandenburg school."

"Good morning, *German Journal*."

"Hi. My name is Tom Hanson, and I'm interested in finding one of your contributors who's an expert on U-boats. Some of my American history students are interested in the subject, and I would like to set up an interview."

"Yes. That's Captain Hans Alder. He's becoming so popular with war buffs that he has an interview schedule with us. Let's see, he left a message. He'll be available tomorrow, Thursday afternoon, at three. You can dial him directly at 305-421-3476 to make an appointment."

I did some homework on the plane, reading whatever I could find in the office about U-boats and their captains. I actually found a photo of a smiling Hans

Alder at an annual reunion of U-boat sailors and their American counterparts, sometimes one having sunk the other.

I arrived on time at the one story ranch style house, a stone's throw from the ocean, with a huge palm tree in the front yard. "Captain Alder. Thank you for seeing me on such short notice."

Alder welcomed me with a smile. "Happy to talk to someone interested in U-boats. Come in, my boy. My wife's out shopping today, so we have the place to ourselves. Have an iced tea. How can I help you?"

Hans Alder's personality was as cheerful as his welcome.

"Some of my students are fascinated by the German U-boat service during the war. It seems they were a very independent and brave bunch of sailors."

"You're right there," Alder said, and he began a discourse about U-boats that lasted for the next twenty minutes. "The U-boat service was ultimately a more dangerous one than we ever expected. Only one-sixth of the boats active in the war survived. 1943 was a terribly bad time for U-boats. Of course, some of us were captured. Not I, but there are stories of US ships picking up survivors of boats they sank."

Refilling our glasses with tea, he continued, "There's also the story my friends told me about the boat captured off the coast of Maine. They like to tease me about how difficult U-boat conditions were. They showed me an article years after the incident about a boat that stopped to pick up some boys and bring them home to Germany. They had come here on the boat, 636 I think it was, and the crossing from Europe terrified the boys. They were involved in combat, of course.

"Well, one boy was so relieved to know he could avoid another three weeks aboard the boat, that he wept hysterically. He would have gone, but was pretty glad he didn't have to. My friends couldn't let that one pass without needling me."

"Seems like it took a special kind of courage for sailors to be in that service," I said.

"I believe so. Glad you recognize that, Tom. Anyway, those crewmen were detained until the end of the war and then sent back to Germany. I expect there are records of the event in US Navy files. I'm not sure what happened to the boys they picked up."

"I wonder if you're familiar with the Brandenburg Commandoes, Sir? Not much information is available about them."

"They were quite a well-trained group, I gather. Worked quietly, but they were very effective. Never met anyone affiliated with them, but I do know they had quite a good reputation for getting the job done. They kept to themselves, were quite secretive.

"So, we're all retired sailors down here now. We get together to share stories over a beer or two. The only thing we fight about is who picks up the bar bill.

"My wife and I moved here in '48. I patrolled this shore during the war, and did my share of damage, but I always made sure survivors were okay before we left. We couldn't pick any up, of course, we were too small, but we gave them water and medical supplies. Some of my best friends here are sailors who were on US ships.

"Well," he said standing. "I hope you have what you came for, Tom."

"Even more than I'd hoped for, Captain Alder. Thank you so much for your hospitality, and your wealth of information. My students will be thrilled to hear your stories."

He shook my hand. "Bring them down next time."

As soon as I returned to the hotel room, I called my office. "Hi Marty, Tom Hanson here. I'm interested in a case from 1943. A German U-boat, maybe number 636, was captured off the Maine coast. Bureau agents interviewed one or two German passengers, maybe involved with sabotage. Since Portland comes under our jurisdiction, I'm hoping the file is there. The Navy may have all the information, but I thought I'd start at home first."

"Since this is a sabotage case, it probably would be File Number 98 something," Marty said. "I'll find whatever we have. If the Navy captured the boat, they'd have any physical evidence that remained on board. Call the US Navy Destroyer Base at Casco Bay. It's a large base bordering Portland. Ships set out to capture a U-boat in Maine would have sailed from there."

"Thanks. I'll be home this afternoon."

It was after five before I got back to the Boston office. "Hey, Larry, Thanks again for your help. I might have something. Captain Alder's terrific. A really delightful guy. We have the first possible glimmer of light in this entire case."

"Glad to help anytime, Tom."

I picked up the hefty file from Marty with the interviews of FBI agents on the incident of capturing a

U-boat, October 28th, 1943, and the arrest of a German saboteur. An evidence box accompanied the reports of the case, but I curbed the temptation to open it until I had more time.

Next day I took the steps necessary to get the report from the Navy. Since the matter was one of national security at the time, I needed to write up a formal request letter with a case title, the file number 98723, the reason for the request, and signatures from my department head and supervisor. The day was gone by the time I had all the documentation.

I made an appointment at Casco Bay for one o'clock the next day, put the documents in my car for tomorrow's trip, and drove home to my condo on Beacon Street. I cooked my favorite macaroni and cheese for dinner, and relaxed with "I love Lucy."

The next afternoon the sailor on duty at Casco Bay handed me the report. "Everything's in order, Sir."

I read: "October 28, 1943. The Casco Bay Destroyer Base, named Sail, was notified that a German U-boat would be in shallow water near a Newport Beach cottage designated by a light in the second floor window at twenty four hundred hours. The mission was to pick up two German saboteurs and transport them back to Germany. Three destroyers were deployed, moving in as the boat surfaced. U-boat 636 was boarded and contained without a shot fired. The captain and crew were transported by destroyer to the brig at Sail. The saboteurs were not among the personnel aboard the boat. U-boat 636 was towed to the Portsmouth Naval Shipyard in New Hampshire, where it remains."

Since I had to go through Portsmouth on the way back to Boston, I stopped by the shipyard to ask about 636. It had been there for several years, but had been vandalized many times, and was finally scuttled. Even with the stop, I beat the commuter traffic on the return trip to Boston. I couldn't wait to get my hands on the interview and evidence box waiting in my office.

The file Marty gathered started with bureau interviews of an American citizen living in Norfolk, Massachusetts. He walked into the Boston bureau office on Saturday, October 23rd, 1943. "I'm Steven Furst," the report quoted. "I've been a German spy, working with DSS, for three years and I'm here to make a bargain. I'll tell you all I know about espionage activities on the east coast in return for my life. I'm aware that aiding persons to cross US borders for sabotage is the same as helping enemy soldiers invade American territory, punishable by death in wartime, but I cannot in good conscience any longer condone what the Nazis are doing to my country."

The agents reported advising him to plead guilty to aiding saboteurs, and to give them all the information he could. In return, they would recommend a prison sentence rather than execution.

Furst admitted to aiding his native Germany by serving as an intelligence currier for DSS, and renting the vacation cottage on Newport Beach to aid in the landing of German saboteurs in August, 1943. Over time he became horrified by the actions of the Nazis and lost heart for his undercover activities.

Furst's testimony was emotional and believable. He was detained and met with agents for the next several days, supplying names of German spies and their whereabouts. He provided keys to several DSS codes, told of places where intelligence was gathered, and where he transported it. Then he confessed everything he knew about the impending October 28th pick up of the two German passengers. The agents enlisted his aid in the seizure of the U-boat.

I spread the items in the evidence box on a table in my office: a duffle bag, phony documents in an American name, Jeffrey Smith, a German Army uniform, and some blasting caps. The pen and pencil set had been refitted as detonation devices. No question what this boy did while he was here. It'll be interesting if he tells all in his statement. No mention of Heinrich Mueller, but the Navy report had said two German saboteurs. These evidence items needed closer scrutiny.

An envelope contained an unidentified capsule, and a leather case held a bronze German Army medal in the shape of a cross with a large Swastika in the center. Under the New Hampshire driver's license were ones from Maine and Vermont with photos of Jeffrey Smith, and a receipt from the Bureau for $4,000 American. This evidence is the equipment of a trained saboteur. Something a Brandenburg Commando might have carried.

I sat at my desk to read the interview with Johann Schmidt concerning his October 28th capture as the proposed passenger on U-boat 636. Schmidt had been at the Furst cottage since late afternoon. Three agents entered the cottage at eleven p.m., one hour before Schmidt's scheduled departure.

Schmidt snatched up the jacket of a German Army Uniform in an effort to declare himself a prisoner of war. As he was being arrested, he became emotional, manic, both crying and laughing. Between sobs he repeated. "No boat! I don't have to get on the boat!"

The agents concealed themselves to wait for the other passenger to appear, but he never did. At midnight they could hear the commotion just off shore as the Navy captured U-boat 636. Two of the agents took Schmidt by car to the Boston Bureau office while the other remained at the cottage with Furst in case the second passenger arrived later.

Schmidt's interrogation began immediately. He refused to say anything except his name until the agents convinced him he'd be executed unless he gave them useful information. He became exceedingly cooperative.

He told them he was trained at Brandenburg. *Yes, I knew it!* He had hit three targets on this trip to America: a bridge abutment in New Hampshire, a railroad crossing on a North/South line in Vermont, and the power supply at a hydroelectric plant in Maine, going into detail about the amount and placement of explosives. He repeated emphatically that the hits were all at night, he didn't hurt any people.

Schmidt remained loyal to his traveling companion, not answering any questions about him until the agents advised him that's the kind of information that would stand in his favor at trial. Johann reported he only knew his friend's German name. The agents encouraged him to tell them honestly whatever he could.

"His name is Heinrich Mueller. We were at Brandenburg together, but I don't know what his mission was here in America."

Jackpot!

I laid the report down on the desk, took a deep breath, and leaned back in the chair. I'd have to be deliberate about how I'd handle things from here. Can't risk tipping my hand to Miller until the time's right.

Incredible! This was here in Boston all the time, but I'd never have looked for evidence about Miller connected with a German U-boat unless Captain Alder had pointed me in that direction. Thank you, Sir.

Clearly Schmidt was ready to board the boat with his duffle bag full of goodies. Wouldn't Miller have had such a bag as well? Where is it? If he had it with him it would have been destroyed in the fire. Susan and Max never mentioned any kind of bag when he tried to get out the window. I'll have to ask them again about Miller's attempt to escape.

The other saboteurs who came to the states by sub, the George Dasch gang in DC, buried their stuff for later retrieval. Could Miller's bag still be at the factory? Buried? Maybe not, with all the renovation to the building and grounds since then, but it's worth the effort to find out. If he didn't have the bag with him, and he was carried out of the building severely injured, then it might still be somewhere on the property.

Time to get a job. Hope I can remember how to drive a box truck. I had a paper route when I was ten, why not now?

Late Saturday afternoon I called Susan. “I have a question for you, and I’d like to tell you about my next step in our dance with Miller. I’m starving. How about a bite to eat while we talk? Somewhere out of town for a change.”

“I know just the place,” she said.

The Roundup in North Oakhill had a western motif, with wait people in fringed leather vests and photos of ranches and cattle drives covering the walls. The lanterns overhead were dim and flickering, suggesting the diners were outside by a campfire.

“The best steaks this side of Boston,” Susan said, “where a hungry man can get a proper dinner.”

It was just five o’clock. Only a few tables were occupied. I asked for one at the back of the room. We ordered, and when Susan had taken a sip of her soda she said, “Can’t wait to hear what you’ve been up to.”

“Well, I need to tell you. I’m going undercover next week.”

Her eyes lit up, “Really? That sounds so spy-movie-ish.”

“Just part of the job. I want to have access to the building and grounds without arousing suspicion. I’m going to apply for a job delivering papers. I hear there’s a big turnover with those guys since it’s not the best working hours, and the paper gets delivered no matter the weather. I’ll dress for the part, but I wanted to warn you to be prepared in case you see me there.”

Susan couldn't help smiling. "I'm so glad you're here. Max and I want to do the right thing, but we don't know what it is, and we couldn't pull it off if we did."

"There's much more work to do," I said, "and I may need your help again at some point, but I'm glad to hear you're feeling more comfortable. By the way, the day of the factory fire, did Miller have a suitcase, or some kind of bag when he tried to get out of the window?"

"No, in fact he used two hands to try to open it, and then he broke it. I'll never forget seeing the knife in his hand, but nothing else." Susan shivered.

"Sorry, I won't bring it up again."

The steaks were perfect, the melt-in-your-mouth variety. Susan mentioned what the cleaning lady had said about her article. "Seems I need that kind of courage boosting to think I may be a writer someday."

"You will be," I said. "And you're brave. It took courage to face those cleaning women and pull off your escape." Susan had to chuckle.

We pulled up to her house. "Thanks for dinner," she said, "I'll let Max know what you're doing. Paul's coming home with his dog tomorrow, so we're going to welcome him. Please tell us if we can help in any way."

"Believe me, I will," I said, and I drove away.

I spent Sunday at home reading the rest of the transcript from Johann Schmidt's interrogation. He offered details about Camp Klein, the trip he and four other boys took to Berlin, and his studies at Brandenburg.

He described his other missions to America, some successful, others not. I concluded from his testimony that Johann's path paralleled Henry's, filling in the five missing years of Henry's record.

I rummaged through my closet for old, worn jeans and tattered work boots, and found a tee shirt with a Chevy logo to wear to apply for my new job. Rather than wait for my beard to grow I donned a fake mustache from another job, and some black-rimmed eyeglasses. Tomorrow I'd get the proper Mass. driver's license with a new photo and a new name.

I made some scrambled eggs for lunch in my new renovated kitchen. The tawny maple cabinets felt warm around me compared to the sterile white ones I had taken out. I felt fortunate to be working and living in Boston. It's a human scale city, inviting residents to walk around the neighborhoods. And the Victorian architecture in the Back Bay reminded me of my father's restorations. The Public Garden at tulip time was breathtaking, and Arthur Fiedler conducted free outdoor concerts at the Hatch Shell on the Fourth of July. Every year I considered inviting friends to join me for the Fourth, but I never did.

My work at the Bureau had always been satisfying, but it was also intense. My home was my escape. I liked being here on my own. I had to admit it, I enjoyed my solitude.

Larry didn't recognize me when I entered the office the next day.

"Need some paperwork done," I said to Phil in the lab. "I need a Mass. CDL license to drive a box truck, and a birth certificate in case they ask for it with the application."

"Sure thing. By the way, Tom. Can you drive a truck?" He raised his eyebrows.

"Yeah, had to learn for another job. Drove interstate. Glad it's coming in handy."

"Okay. What's your name?"

"Jeffrey Roberts. Born in Bellville, Nova Scotia, Canada."

"You got it. Let's get a photo. Keep the glasses on." I sat on the stool as Phil switched on the floor lamp, aimed it at my face, and adjusted the camera to shoot my photo. A few signatures here and there, and ten minutes later I was a different person.

Back in my office, I took a closer look at the contents of Schmidt's bag. The receipt for $4,000 intrigued me. That's how much Schmidt had left after being here for about three months. Henry's attack at the factory happened just after he and Johann arrived. His bag would have considerably more cash, making it quite attractive to anyone who discovered it.

Mr. Cain at the *Chronicle* greeted Jeff Roberts cheerfully, happy to see an applicant for a driver's job. "Looks like everything's in order, Mr. Roberts," he said.

"Call me Jeff. Mr. Roberts is my dad."

"Can you start tonight?"

"The sooner the better," I said with a grin. "Bills are waiting to be paid."

"Great. Come in about midnight to bundle the paper and load the truck. You should be back by six or so. I can give you a copy of your route now to study, and a key to the back door. You'll be driving truck Number 3. Sometimes there will be supplements to insert into the papers. You can go out back now to give the truck a test drive. They're very comfortable, like sitting in your living room."

"Thanks, Mr. Cain."

I drove Number 3 out of the parking lot, up Chapman, and onto Main Street. Just like riding a bike. I'll put some miles on every night with this route. Might be fun.

I looked around when I returned to the parking lot. There had to be extensive excavation to construct this huge asphalt surface right up to the building's loading dock. There is some landscaped ground around it, but that's fifty feet away, too far for Miller. If the bag had been buried, it's not in this parking lot.

Those concrete steps from the exterior door weren't there then. The form for the steps and the landing would be supported by a deep slab under the bottom step. With the four-by-four foot platform at the door, and three steps, the slab would be at least six feet from the building. If Henry were to dig a hole, he'd do it closer, maybe under where the steps are now.

Chapman Street is too close to the building on the other side. What about the stand of blue spruce trees between the building and the gas station? Huge roots are there now, but it might have been a possibility then.

It's not reasonable to think the bag could be inside the building. Fire consumed the main floor of the factory, and Miller didn't have it when he tried to leave. If it was still here, the most logical places were either under the stairs to the dock, or in the stand of spruces.

To ease the logistics of traveling back and forth to Boston, I booked a room at the Eagle Motel in Oakhill and stocked it with work clothes. Then I called Police Chief Engels and Susan to tell them how to reach me. Just to be sure, in the next few days, I poked into the landscaped area behind the *Chronicle* building. I found nothing. Of course a construction worker might have found it sixteen years ago during the renovation of the property. What would he have done with it? Taken the money for sure.

Time to do more digging, but I could never fit into the space under the steps. I'll need an accomplice.

Susan's phone was ringing as she unlocked the door to her apartment after dinner with Tom Hanson on Saturday afternoon. "Hi Susan, it's Michael. I've been here visiting my parents, and I'm just leaving to go back into town. I wondered if you'd like to go for a coffee?"

"Sure, but this time I'll cook. Coffee's about the only thing I can do well."

The pot was just starting to perk when Michael arrived. "Hi. Come in. Coffee's almost ready. Let's sit on the sofa. I'll get us some cups."

Settled on the tiny wicker sofa with their coffee, Michael said, "I'm really glad we took this time to get to know each other again. I'm comfortable with you. You make me laugh. Sometimes it's not easy for me to relax, but you have the magic for that."

"I think we just like the same things, so it's comfortable to talk about them."

When she put her cup on the glass-topped wicker coffee table, he did too. He reached his arms around her, stroked a stray wisp of hair off her forehead, and said, "I've been wondering something for a while. I wonder how you'd like living in Boston ... maybe working for the *Globe* or some of the publishing houses, or just doing some writing. Fact is, I think about you all the time. I remember us walking through the Public Garden, and the day we went shopping on Newbury Street. Wherever I go, I'd like you to be there too."

"Wow. That's the sweetest thing anyone has ever said to me."

"I think I hear a 'but' coming."

"I'll have to take some time to think about it. I mean, I haven't been alone long enough to figure out what I want. Maybe someday it could happen, but it's too soon for me to make that decision."

"Good thing I'm a patient man." He kissed her forehead and then her lips. "The best things in life are worth waiting for."

14

Shasta

Max and Paul found Shasta at a German shepherd breeder on the shore in Davenport. She ran to Paul asking for pats as soon as the breeder walked her into the visiting room. Her face was delicate for a shepherd, black with light brown marks above her eyes, her ears were erect, and her soft brown eyes were alert.

"This is my dog." Paul grinned up at Max.

"She's gorgeous," Max said.

"We'll send her to the farm in Connecticut for two weeks to be trained on her own," the breeder said. "Then you'll go down for three days so she'll learn to obey the commands from you. Will that work for you, Mr. Pietrowski?"

"Absolutely. Please call me Paul. I can't wait to get her home."

Shasta's training would include all the common commands dogs need to learn for safety, as well as ones to protect Paul. "Once she's trained," the breeder told them, "her first encounter with an intruder will be to bark and hold, keeping him in one place until you give her a command, Paul. If the person she's holding moves or challenges her in any way, she'll bite and hold. Believe me, those jaws can do some serious damage.

"She'll fight to the death to keep you from harm. Of course, as soon as you command her to stop, she will, and she'll be playful and affectionate with you and anyone who's welcome into your home. She's from wonderful stock. Some of her siblings will be working with police departments."

The next order of business for Paul was to replenish his kitchen supplies. He and Katherine went shopping at his favorite specialty shops on the north shore. They found a new restaurant supply store with a retail space selling, "every conceivable kitchen gadget," Paul said.

While he was in Connecticut training with Shasta, Max had the cabin outfitted with hefty deadbolt locks on the doors, knowing Paul would want to go home as soon as he returned with her. He wished the cabin weren't so isolated. Maybe if he asked to spend some vacation time fishing before school starts Paul would agree to let him stay there for a while.

Susan called Max a few days after she and Tom had bugged Miller's phone. "Hi Sue. How did it go the other night at Miller's office?"

"Great. There's something I think you should know."

"I'm just about to leave for school to pick up some books. Can I come by your house?"

"Sure. See you in a while."

As soon as Max stepped through the door, Susan showed him a photo in the *Chronicle* of the Oakhill School Board for next year, and an announcement of their first meeting scheduled for August 23rd.

"Max, he must know who you are. Otherwise why would Henry Miller be the newest member of the Oakhill School Board?"

"I don't think he's that interested in education." Max took the paper and sat on the sofa to read the article. "I've learned to trust your intuition, Sue. I think you're right. Incredible. Now he's my boss too."

"Can he do anything to you in that position?"

"Not unless I foul up badly, and I have no intention of doing that ... I love my job. I'll be sure to read the boring minutes of the school board meetings this year. At least you're still safe. He doesn't know about you yet."

"Matter of time," she said, sitting in the chair opposite him. "He's better at this than we are. He's a trained saboteur. We don't have the slightest idea how to deal with him."

"My focus right now is on Paul," Max said. "But, wait a minute. If Miller knows who I am, maybe it's not a good idea for me to be with Paul after all. He might try to get two birds with one stone."

"I think you should let Tom know about this, Max. Let's call him."

Max walked to the kitchen, dialed the phone on the wall near the doorway, and faced into the living room to include Susan in the conversation. After telling him about Miller's appointment, Tom said, "Okay. That's a pretty good clue about how he intends to approach you. Think about whether there might be anything negative he could dig up on you in regard to school. Is there anyone you've annoyed, or rules you've broken, even accidentally. If you come up with anything please tell me about it."

"Has the bug turned anything up yet?"

"Not yet, but I'll keep digging. Meanwhile, thanks for the information, and keep in touch."

Max slumped onto the sofa, lowered his head, and raked his hands through his hair.

"Want a coffee?" Susan asked.

"Yeah, that'd be great. My job, Sue. It's the best part of my life."

"We'll see this through, Max." She went to the kitchen for the pot, filled two mugs on the coffee table with the steaming liquid, and sat in the chair. "It feels like he has the upper hand now, but he'll be caught and punished. I know it."

"Tom said he'd keep digging for leads. Right now I'd grab at any straw. How did it go the other night at the paper? Did you feel like a kid breaking into the boxes again?"

"It went well. Some cleaning people interrupted us, but Tom stayed calm, and got us out of a sticky situation. I told him how relieved I felt that someone else knew about our secret"

"I do too. I trust Tom. I've thought so many times about what might have happened if we'd just told an adult then. Some of this awful mess might have been avoided if I hadn't been so scared of my dad."

"Don't do that, Max. None of this is your fault. The violence happened to us. We were children. Whether we told about it or not doesn't change that. He did it, not you."

"Miller or my dad?"

"Both. What did the doctor say about telling Paul?"

"Just what we expected. He stopped me part way through to say this news might make Paul regress to a safer place in his mind and stall his recovery. I certainly don't want that."

"When is he coming home with Shasta?"

"Sunday afternoon. Want to go with me to welcome him?"

"Yeah, I'd love to. Listen, Max, please don't start worrying and getting fearful. We're in this together. You, Tom and I will come up with something that works. Remember how angry you were the day Miller called Paul. Go there again. That's a good kind of anger. It's energizing. I don't want to have to start picking you up again." They both chuckled as he left.

Max's dinner was waiting for him when he arrived home. Katherine filled a bowl with the beef stew she'd prepared and asked, "Where did you go? I called the office and you weren't there."

"I stopped at Susan's to tell her about Paul and the dog coming home on Sunday. She'd like to rekindle their friendship."

"I'm so glad he's getting the dog," Katherine said. "He's isolated up there at Craggy. We'll all feel that he's safer. Then perhaps you won't have to spend so much time with him and Susan. Truth is, I've been meaning to bring this up for a while, and now it's happened again. Seems this is the right time.

"You've been stopping at Susan's an awful lot lately. I think you spend more time with her than you do with me. I'm feeling left out of your life lately. You've taken a different turn, and it's away from me. You don't seem to need me anymore."

Max looked up, raising his eyebrows. "Sure I do. I've been feeling better about going off on my own, but that's good, it shows I'm beating this disease. But you're my wife, Katherine. Of course I need you."

"You know," she said, "my parents were the models for the way we've decided to live. My mom helped support my dad with his panic attacks, and they've had thirty-five years of a great marriage. I believed it'd be the same for us, but I've been feeling very lonely for a while now, and I don't like it."

The obvious solution flashed into Max's mind. He lowered his head and turned away to avoid her eyes. Katherine would understand why I'm spending so much time with Susan if she knew the reason, but how can I tell her about the day at the boxes? I vowed to keep it a secret. In fact, I was the one who insisted we all agree never to tell, and Susan hasn't. I don't want to violate Susan's trust and betray our promise, but Katherine has a right to know why I'm behaving this way ... I only hope this is the right thing to do.

He looked up at her again. "Okay. Maybe it's time I told you something. I'm breaking a long-term vow to do it, but it might help you understand."

Taking her hands in his, he sat down with her at the table. Looking into her eyes, he began, "See, Susan, Paul, and I were involved in a violent incident when we were kids. We were playing in a place we called 'the boxes', and there was an explosion. We didn't cause the explosion, but we know who did. We swore to keep it a secret, never to tell anyone, and none of us has. But the person who created the violence has returned to Oakhill, and we're trying to figure out a way to get rid of him. That's why I've been spending so much time with Sue and Paul."

After a beat of silence, Katherine said, "Unbelievable!" Sitting straight back in her chair, and taking another moment she said, "You and Susan have a secret? Do you believe telling me you've shared a major secret with another woman, but kept it from me for all the years we've been together, will make me accept your behavior? It doesn't! In fact, it makes me wonder what else I don't know about you. I wonder if I know you at all."

"But I thought if you knew—"

"What about the vows you made to me when we got married?"

"Unfair, Katherine. I've always honored you."

"Is this how you honor me? By keeping a promise you made to another woman? Is that vow more important than the ones you made to me? I guess it is! Look, I gave up my nursing career to support you full time, and I admit I loved doing it. But this is not working anymore." She walked to the sink, clenched her fists, and pounded them on the counter. "How dare you treat me like an outsider. Keeping secrets all this time ... with Susan. I've been betrayed."

"Katherine, no you haven't. I'd never betray you." I fumbled, raking my fingers through my hair, wondering how I could convince her nothing happened between me and Susan except for a childhood promise. But she didn't give me a chance to speak.

"I've devoted myself to making your life comfortable, possible even, and now you're a successful teacher. What benefits are left in this relationship for me? I need some distance to find out if this is how I want to spend the rest of my life. I need to leave here."

"C'mon Katherine. You're overreacting. My childhood promise isn't a threat to our marriage." I walked up behind her and put my hands on her arms to turn her around, but she twisted away, moving to the table.

"We had a good marriage once," she said, "some tenderness at the beginning, but you've changed. You don't need me like you did then. You're not grateful for my help anymore. I'm being pushed out ... by Susan! No, I need to get away from here, to find out who I am besides Max Pietrowski's caretaker!"

My stomach clenched. I couldn't believe her stinging words. "How can you speak to me like that? How long have you felt this resentment?"

"Okay, I've decided. I'm going to spend a few days at my mother's. I need a break from us to think. Please give me the car keys."

He reached into his pocket, considering whether he should let her have the keys or not. Clutching them he held on for a moment, wondering what he could say to deter her. But she stood her ground, chin up, defiant in front of him. He surrendered, putting the keys on the table.

Grabbing the keys and her purse, she turned and left without another word.

What just happened here? Katherine's gone to her mother's. I guess I shouldn't have told her about the boxes. I made a choice, the wrong one. I've made everything worse. How will I get through the day? I'm alone. What if...a thousand things could happen.

Stop it! This is real. Deal with it!

Okay, take a breath. The therapist said I can decide what I think about, can choose what I pay attention to. If I learn to recognize those panic-causing thoughts, I can replace them with relaxing ones. I'll rest in my recliner, calm my mind and body. What were his words? I need to "see my world as it is, not as I fear it might be."

Changing my thinking, now that's an exhilarating goal. I wonder if it's the way I can finally face my terrors and contain them.

He slid back into the chair, pushed it to recline, and closed his eyes. He took deep breaths. Okay, now, Mr. Ski, relax. Come to think of it, I'm most relaxed with my kids in the classroom. Maybe that's a clue. Maybe

I should practice listening to people the way I do with them, looking beyond myself. I'm fed up with who I am right now for sure.

Let's see. This is Thursday. There's enough food in the house to get through the weekend, I'll need a used car to get around, and Monday's ordeal will be a trip to Oakhill Grocery. Hold on. Think through one thing at a time, slowly.

Silly, but I feel a little giddy. My music!

He put on his favorite Tchaikovsky record and turned the volume up loud. He was hungry. The fat from the meat in the beef stew had congealed and was floating on the surface of the liquid. He tossed it out, made a big hamburger with onions, and washed it down with a bottle of beer.

This is weird. I'm sure I love my wife, but I feel ... free. Maybe that's a typical reaction when two people split, like losing weight. It may be fleeting, or false, but I have to explore this feeling.

Friday and Saturday he did small jobs around the house, weeding the gardens and mowing the lawn, all with his favorite music spilling through the open windows. Saturday night he contemplated calling Katherine.

Sometimes he forgot she had left. He expected to see her when he walked into the kitchen, then he'd remember. The scent of her cologne lingered on the pillow beside him in bed. Yet, he continued to feel, what? Relief? Weightless? Should he be guilty having these feelings? Was he being disloyal to Katherine? But he didn't feel guilty. His feelings were real. He decided to wait a day to call. He didn't want to press her too soon.

Maybe this is an opportunity. My chance to prove to myself that I'm overcoming my problem. I'll take things a little slowly at first, but Katherine's action may be the kick I need to beat my constant fear of being afraid, to lick these demons that have controlled me for so long.

On Sunday morning he called Susan. "Hi, still planning to go to Paul's?"

"Sure am."

"Well, could you pick me up?"

"Oh no, Max. Did you have an attack?"

"No, nothing like that, but Katherine left with the car. I'll tell you on the way."

In the car Max described the incident with Katherine and said, "I don't get it. I'm blindsided. She left me, after I explained things to her."

"Max, sometimes I think you're naïve. Remember how annoyed I got when you told me about the man being German and that you took his knife? I want to know I have all the information about an important matter, with nothing left out. Can you see that keeping a life-changing secret from your wife feels like a worse offense than leaving her alone from time to time? I might have reacted the same way Katherine did."

"There's something else," he said. "I'm not sad. I think I should be, but what I'm feeling is free. I don't think it's normal."

"Whatever you feel is normal for you. There are no shoulds with feelings. They just are. I'm impressed you're paying attention to your emotions, but please don't second-guess them. Sometimes I think they're the most important data we have. They're what make us human.

"And, Katherine may be feeling less indispensable to you now that you're more confident. You'll just have to work out a new way of being together. Give her a few more days to cool off, and then be very sweet, promising to keep her totally informed. I bet she'll come rushing back. Know that I'm here if you'd like to talk, okay?"

"Okay. Thanks, Sue."

"Y'know, sometimes I wonder how come I have such clear insight into other people's lives, but my own is a total mystery to me. I have to start taking the advice I just gave you, to start trusting my feelings instead of trying to figure everything out.

"Oh, I talked to Tom last night. He went out of town for a few days, but he's back. He's going undercover at the paper so he can explore the property, and he thought I should know in case I bumped into him. I don't know if his trip had anything to do with us, but I'm sure he'll tell us in his own time."

Shasta's deep bark greeted them as they drove up to Paul's porch. Then it stopped as abruptly as it started. "He must have corrected her when he saw us," Max said.

"Scared me," Susan said. "Better than an alarm."

By the time Paul opened the door, Shasta's tail wagged so hard it seemed to go in circles.

"How do you like my new doorbell?" he asked.

"She's beautiful." Susan gave Shasta a scratch behind the ear. "And very effective."

"Come into the kitchen. Didn't they do a terrific job? You'd never know anything bad happened." Shasta hugged Paul's side as they walked into the kitchen, and lay down beside his chair.

"I had the carpenter install dead bolts on the doors when he repaired the damage," Max said. "Hope you don't mind."

"Not at all. Good idea. Have some cookies. Good to see you again, Susan."

They chatted about the new recipes Paul had created, and his interest in visiting the English countryside as the setting for a new book of poems. After a pleasant visit Susan drove Max through Tim's Used Car Lot to see what he might find to use while Katherine stayed at her mother's.

"I'm pleased, and surprised, that Paul didn't seem at all uncomfortable about being in the house again," Susan said.

"I am too. Maybe it's because Shasta's there."

"Do you want to go anywhere while you have wheels?"

"Not today, but tomorrow it'd be great if you could bring me back to Tim's so I can pick up a car."

"Will do," she said as she drove up Max's driveway. "And don't worry. She'll come back after realizing what's at stake," With a reassuring smile, she left saying, "See you tomorrow."

···❖···

When Susan took him to Tim's Used Car Lot, Max fell in love.

A 1956 Chevrolet Bel Air black and ivory rag top convertible enthralled and captivated him. With the top down, it was the sleekest thing he'd ever seen. The rich black body sported a streak of ivory starting at the front fender, gradually increasing until it exploded into a completely ivory back end. The ivory upholstery had black v-shaped inserts on each of the four seat backs. The paint had a few dings, and it wasn't the practical car he should buy, but it was gorgeous. He couldn't resist.

He bargained with Tim, buying it for a price he could afford. With a temporary plate to get it home, he took Susan for a ride, feeling like a kid at Christmas.

"This is so much fun," she said. "Not at all like you."

"But I don't know what I'm like. I've been protecting myself for so long from everything that might set off an attack I haven't really been living, except in class. I only know this feels great."

He stopped at Oakhill Center Grocery, bought the few things he needed, and drove Susan back to Tim's for her car. He couldn't stop grinning.

"That's the first time I've been in Oakhill Grocery in eight years," he said. "I cheated by taking you with me, but I'm sure I'd be okay on my own. Think I'll go home and wash my car."

"Keep in touch," Susan said, "and congratulations on your new baby."

15

Max's Quest

I'm ready for battle. At the kitchen table, armed with legal size pads of paper and fine tipped pens, I decided to attack my Agoraphobia Immunity Program the same way I'd plan a program of study for my students. I have the central challenge: Paralyzing Fear. What integration of goals, strategies, activities, and experiences could I develop to address the problem?

First I'll adjust my attitude from defensive to offensive. I can no longer spend precious energy avoiding situations. Instead I'll encounter them in manageable doses. One activity will be driving to a crowded place, and getting out of the car. Maybe that's two steps.

Experiences will include attending an event I enjoy, like a concert. I'll direct my mind to focus only on the music, blocking out the environment. Another will be driving to the beach, maybe to the Cape, even though that means going over a high bridge. It'll be a tough test. I need to remind myself that no bridges have fallen down lately, and I can stay on the inside lane. No need for heroics, just for progress.

Write it down.

Okay, I've got a pretty good list of goals and activities. If this were an academic program I'd have a demonstration to share my learning. My drive to the beach can be my Performing Knowledge presentation.

The campaign begins. Is it excitement or anxiety flipping my stomach? It's a risk. I'll be crushed if I fail. I could chuck the whole idea right now. Who will know if I don't try?

I'll know, that's who. My life is in my hands. I need to take this shot. Win or lose I'll give it my all. It's my mettle that's being tested. I need a motto, a battle cry. "Just Start!" Yes!

Katherine had been gone a week when I called her. I miss her. I do. But Susan had the right idea. We'll have to work out a new way of being together when she comes home."I'm sorry," her mother said, "but Katherine isn't at home. She's at BC. She enrolled in a summer nursing course. It's good to hear from you, Max. I'll tell her you called."

An hour later Katherine called back. "Hi, Max. Mom said you called."

"I did. She told me about your class. That's great."

"Yeah, I was lucky to get into in at the last moment. So much has changed since the last courses I took that it's like learning everything all over again, but I loved it then and I still do."

"Will you work at St Michael's when you're finished?"

"Probably not. The most cutting edge techniques are being done in the Boston hospitals. I visited Bradley the other day. The innovative things they're doing are so impressive. That's where I'd like to work."

"Have you given any thought to us?"

"I have. I think we need to stay apart for a while, so each of us can decide what's best. I've been busy. I'm loving what I'm doing, and I'm not ready to go back to what we had."

"I'm glad to hear you say that, because I'm not either. I'm hoping we can work out a new way of being married. You could go back to the work you love in Boston, and I can be more independent. We'd be happier than ever."

"I'm not ready to discuss that possibility. I need to explore what's best for me right now. That seems to be more study and meaningful work. I need to be on my own to focus. I hope you can understand, Max."

"I understand you've distanced yourself from me, and that's how you want it to be," I said with more of an edge than I'd planned.

"Let's not argue, Max. I'll call you again in a few weeks. Goodbye." She hung up.

I've just been dumped. Clearly she's not coming back. I'm surprised she didn't even ask what I meant about being independent. I guess she's not interested enough to find out. Think I'll take my first trip to the library alone.

···❖···

Can't believe it's two weeks into my program. Wish I could tell someone, but I need to do this on my own. I've done at least one of my activities every day. Can't say I wasn't fearful, like the day I drove to the mall. Took care of myself by finding a parking spot hugging the store, but I sat there twenty minutes before I could get out. I remember the sensation that the environment and my body were not real, like I was in a scene in a movie.

Music on the radio calmed me be back to reality. I had to fight the temptation to turn around and go home. After all, no one would know. But I stopped those thoughts and remembered my motto. Just Start. I willed myself to grab the door handle, pull it, and get out of the car. I walked into the music store, and bought the last Patsy Cline and the latest Roy Orbison records. What a Fourth of July feeling. There should have been a parade, church bells ringing. That victory kept me going for days.

I had dinner with Paul twice, and called Susan to see if she had heard anything about the case from Tom, but I didn't tell either of them about my activities. I wasn't ready to reveal my quest yet.

Driving my car was pure joy. The splendid machine responded to my slightest touch. I bought a new AM/FM radio for it, and couldn't help singing along with the music. I remembered my adolescent psyche class at BC, and put myself at the developmental level of a teenager, like my kids at school.

In the kitchen at home I grabbed a wooden spoon from its cylinder on the counter, raised it sword-like and shouted, "Just Start!" Then I had a good laugh at how silly I must look. But this war was serious, as real to me as any of the ones my kids studied.

In time, I could recognize when I distorted my view of events, and exaggerated my feelings. I learned to stop, calm myself, and redirect my thoughts. With any luck I would beat my emotional demons, once and for all.

16

The Black Dragon

But a real demon was waiting just around the corner. *I love anniversaries.* Henry sat at his breakfast table with coffee and toast, August 16, 1961. *They're so nostalgic and sentimental. I can hardly wait to deliver my eighteen-year anniversary gift.*

Later that night at Paul's cabin, Shasta growled, teeth bared, ears back. Grrrrr! Grrrrr!

"Shasta, go back to sleep."

But she nudged his shoulder, persistently, barking in strange yips. *She must need to go out.* Paul pushed back the sheet. Rolling to the side of the bed he opened his eyes. "It's light already. Must be morning." But the light in the room didn't look right. And something assaulted his nose, biting, like smoke. "Something's burning," he said. Shasta danced around, yipping. "Okay, girl. I'm coming."

He got up and glanced out the open window. Churning orange curls of fire were eating the oaks at the top of the hill, reaching into the black sky. Trees not yet engulfed were silhouetted against the white-hot center of the blaze. Branches cracked, snapping off their trees. A whoosh of fire-generated wind propelled a wall of grey smoke rolling toward the cabin.

Paul slammed the window shut, as if it might keep the smoke and fire away. Then he jumped back with a gasp as a hemlock on the hill exploded into flames. He pulled open the bedside table drawer, grabbed the flashlight, and gave Shasta a quick scratch behind her ear. "You're the best dog in the world, girl. let's get out of here."

In the living room he took half a moment to call the fire department. "Paul Pietrowski here. There's a fire in the woods on Craggy Pond. I can't maneuver the driveway from my house. I'm taking my dog to the pond and I'll canoe to the inlet."

He dared one last peek through the bedroom door and out the window. He wished he hadn't. The fire crept closer in just those few moments. Clad in his pajama bottoms and a tee shirt, with Shasta at his heel, he dashed barefoot out the front door and scrambled down the hill to the pond. His heart pounded in his ears. His body felt heavy. No matter how he tried to rush, it seemed he moved in slow motion.

At the beach he flipped the canoe upright and dragged it the few feet to the water's edge. Holding it steady, he waved Shasta in, pushed off, and at last they were out on the pond. He took a deep breath and exhaled. The paddle to the inlet would be slow, but they were safe on the water.

The screeching of her telephone woke Susan in the middle of a dream. "Hello?"

"Susan. It's Max."

"What is it? It's the middle of the night."

"I know, I'm sorry to wake you, but Paul's in trouble. There's a fire at Craggy. He left the cabin and he's canoeing to the inlet. Will you come with me? You're so much better than I am at comforting him."

"Of course. Pick me up on the way."

Susan was surprised to find a crowd when they reached the pond. A reporter and photographer she recognized from the *Chronicle* were there, as well as two Oakhill police officers, an ambulance driver, and Tom had just arrived.

Tom slid toward her and Max. "Get Paul away from here as quickly as possible without saying a word."

Susan began to tremble. Max put his jacket around her shoulders as she whispered, "It's August 16th."

As the canoe touched the shore bottom, Max grabbed it, pulled it up, and said to Paul, "Please let's not say anything until we're in my car, okay?"

"Absolutely."

Susan and Max ignored the photographer who had already started shooting, hurried Paul and Shasta into the car, and Max drove home. He took Paul upstairs to find a sweatshirt and slippers while Susan gave Shasta a bowl of water. The doorbell rang. "I'll go," she said. "Come in, Tom. Time for you to meet Paul."

"Thanks. I went back to Craggy, but I couldn't get close. It's an inferno. Can I use the phone?"

"Hi, Tom," Max said, coming down the stairs with Paul. He ushered everyone into the kitchen and they sat at the table. "This is Tom Hanson, Paul."

"Good to meet you. How are you, Paul?"

"I'm fine, thanks to my pal, Shasta. She woke me and wouldn't stop yipping until I got up. She saved my life." Paul choked back a sob with those words. The enormity of the situation caught up with him.

"Tom's helping us catch the person who's been harassing you," Max said. "The fire may not be related to the other events, but it may, so Tom will help work that out."

"Thanks Tom. Nice to meet you. I appreciate your help," Paul said, more calmly.

Susan offered Tom a mug of coffee, and directed him to the wall phone. He called his foreman at the *Chronicle* to let him know he wouldn't be in for work. Then he listened with Max and Susan as Paul told them of Shasta's insistence that he wake up and their escape from the cabin. "She's the best dog in the world," Paul said.

"I'll be in the neighborhood tomorrow," Tom said. "We're keeping people out of the area for their safety."

"Good idea," Max said. "Paul can stay here with me until it's safe to go home."

Susan made Paul a cup of cocoa, staying close by him. He'd forgotten, but she recalled the other August 16th in 1943, when she had brushed the soaking wet strands of hair out of his eyes in that torrential rainstorm. Miller has traumatized us again. She shuddered. Except for his dog, Paul might have been killed.

"Thanks for the coffee," Tom said. "I may see you tomorrow. Meanwhile, everyone is safe. Get some sleep, and Paul, kudos to Shasta for a good night's work."

"Thanks," Paul headed for the stairs. "See you later."

Susan and Max walked Tom to the door. "Do you know what day it is?" Max asked.

"I do. Criminals love anniversaries. He's being brazenly typical. Time to rein him in. Keep Paul near you."

"I will. Tom, please let me help catch this guy. I'm beyond furious, but I promise I'll keep my emotions in check if you'll let me help. I need to know I'm doing something to protect my little brother."

"I know just what you can do. Susan, can we meet at your place tomorrow?" Tom glanced at his watch. "Oh, it's already tomorrow, so later today, say around two this afternoon? I should have more information by then."

"Absolutely," Susan said. Max grinned.

"I'll go back to Craggy in the morning. Maybe I can get closer. See you both later."

"Mr. Miller," Tony said. "Sorry to call you so late, but Fred Corbin has an article and photos that I think are important enough to go on the front page. He didn't shout, 'Stop the presses!' like in the movies, but that's how I felt when he showed me what he had. Of course, we need your permission to change the layout of page one."

"What's the story, Tony?"

"Fred's headline reads: 'Poet Escapes Forest Fire at Craggy Pond.' There's a huge fire at Craggy right now. Paul Pietrowski had to canoe to the inlet to escape. Fred wrote a short article, and the photo's great."

"I agree, that's front page news. Put the story and photo above the fold so it won't be missed. Good work, Tony."

When he picked up his paper the next morning Henry couldn't help but grin. In the shot Fred used, Paul was stepping out of the canoe with Max's arm around his shoulders, both back to the camera. In the foreground, Paul's dog trotted through a few inches of water. A woman stood across from them, facing the camera.

He recognized her. Susan something, the girl who does local color stories. Miles, that's it, Susan Miles. Now what would she be doing in the middle of the night helping the Pietrowski brothers in a crisis? If I squint I can see the pigtails in her hair.

There they are! All three characters playing Guard the Castle. I'll have to clip the photo as a memento of the night The Black Dragon burned down the forest. But no one knows I'm even remotely involved. I'm a pillar of the community. There are no links to me and I will leave none, except for the ones I've left on purpose. And only the players know the significance of those.

17

Gold Strike

Susan brought out iced coffee and oatmeal cookies for her afternoon guests. "I needed to keep busy this morning so I cooked. The cookies aren't as good as Paul's, but humor me and have one."

"First, the fire," Tom said. "The official story is that someone carelessly tossed a cigarette out of a car window and started the blaze. Couldn't have happened. There were no dead leaves on the ground or other debris that would have ignited before a cigarette extinguished. A person with knowledge of incendiaries started that fire ... someone who has the skill to make a device that would burn hot for at least ten minutes to ignite the underbrush. It would then burn itself out, leaving no trace.

"We know who that person is," Max said.

"True. I found this evidence left in the gravel at the side of the road. It would mean nothing to the police looking for arson."

He removed an envelope from his pocket and dumped three red-tipped black feathers on the table. Susan shrieked, raising her hand to her mouth.

"I'm sorry, Sue, I should have warned you," Tom said.

"It's okay. We know he did it. Dragons set fires. It's just so shocking to see the proof. Of course, that's the reaction he wants from us."

"I walked to the edge of the burn this morning. It didn't jump the driveway to reach Paul's house, but I believe he could have been taken down by the smoke if he didn't get out of there when he did," Tom said.

"I could smell it when I went outside this morning for the mail," Susan said. "Smells like everyone in town has their wood stoves burning."

"Yeah." Max nibbled his cookie. "The humid weather keeps it hanging around, but the first rainy or windy day will help. By the way, Sue, did you see the paper today?"

"I did. So now he knows who I am. Tom, should I quit my job?"

"No. You don't have to go to the office anyway. Don't let him know anything's different. I'll catch you up on what I know so far."

Tom reported on his trip to Florida and the lead from Captain Alder, the FBI interviews, and the evidence in Johann Schmidt's duffle bag. "So, we know Miller is our saboteur. If we could find the duffle bag he had like Johann's, we'd nail him on a serious charge.

"Last week I called in a retired jockey, George Davis. He worked with the Bureau on an interstate horse racing fraud case years ago, and then became an agent.

He's on the road now checking hardware stores to find out who might have bought the items for the incendiary device.

"I asked for George's help because he's a small guy. He crawled into the space under the steps at the *Chronicle* loading dock last Saturday night and prodded every inch to see if Miller's bag might be buried there. No luck. This is where you come in, Max."

"Anything at all."

"Well, the former owners of the *Chronicle*, the Berkeleys, renovated the building in 1945. Shortly after completing the project, Mr. Berkeley became seriously ill, and died within six months. Mrs. Berkeley was more than capable of running the paper, and she did until the sale to *City News*. On the off chance that a construction worker might have found the bag and brought it to the Berkeleys, well, a history teacher would be interested in such a find.

"It's a long shot. So much time has passed and so many people have had access to the property that—"

"I'll do it," Max interrupted. "I'll make an appointment for next week. Thank you, Tom."

"Great. The only other thing I can do as Jeff Roberts is search Miller's office, but I don't think he'd be careless enough to bring anything inside. If we can't turn up his bag, there is another ploy we can use. But, one thing at a time."

Susan walked Tom to the door. "Thank you for letting Max help. It means so much to him."

"Let me know whether he finds anything or not."

"I will," she said.

As soon as Tom left, Max called Mrs. Berkeley. "I'm sorry, Mr. Pietrowski," the housekeeper said. "Mrs. Berkeley's not here. She's at her summer home in Dennis for the month of August, until after Labor Day."

"Do you think she'd mind if I talked to her there? My students would be fascinated by a discovery from the war. I'd like to follow up with her."

"No, I don't think she'd mind. She's always interested in helping educational projects. Tell you what, give me your number and I'll talk to her today. If she's open to speaking with you before she gets back, she'll call."

"That's great. My home phone number is 555-8790. I'll be waiting for her call. Thank you."

Less than an hour later Max's phone rang. "Mr. Pietrowski. How good to hear from you. I see your sister Maria every week except for the month of August. Wish I could take her down here with me. She's told me so much about you. I know how devoted you are to your students."

"Thanks, Mrs. Berkeley. I'm curious about something that may have been found during the renovation of the *Chronicle* property. It may have ended up in your hands. It's a duffle bag that belonged to a World War Two soldier."

"You know, I do recall the contractor bringing a dilapidated canvas bag to the house. He said it might be from the war. I accepted it because of Howard's interest in collecting war memorabilia. It looked frightfully dirty and buggy. I wouldn't allow it in the house, but I remember telling the workman to put it in the shed until my husband could take a look at it. Of course, he passed on shortly thereafter, and I forgot about the thing. Heavens, do you think it might still be there after all these years? I did intend to throw it out, but I focused all my attention on my husband at the time, and I don't recall if I did or not."

"Could I take a look when you come home? It'll be after school starts, but I'll wait."

"Nonsense. I'll tell my housekeeper to let you into the shed right away. She can point out where it might be if it's still there. Now I'm curious myself. Please let me know what you find. My interest is piqued."

"Of course. Thank you for being so kind. I'll keep in touch."

The shed had to be at least a hundred years old. An accumulation of stuff filled the space. An antique rocker with no seat, some rusty fireplace equipment, a rolled up piece of carpet, boxes of moldy books, and a box of trophies from someone's high school days were treasures too dear to toss out. Gesturing to the far corner, the housekeeper said, "The things from the renovation would be over there if you can make your way to it."

"I will." Max said, moving pieces to create a path.

After twenty minutes of finding nothing resembling a duffle bag, he touched a piece of fabric that disintegrated in his hand. He took a closer look. A fabric bag with leather handles looked like it had been the nest of generations of mice. He didn't dare pick it up, but carefully opened it to look inside. He gagged at the stench rising from the interior. Whatever papers had been there were stuck together with mold, or chewed into nest material. Clumps of mouse poop and brown stains decorated the edges of the opening. Prying the top open just a bit more he alerted some sleeping insects that scampered off to darker crannies. He spied something darkly metal, a pistol, and the remains of a uniform jacket. On the collar was a red medal with an eagle clutching ... a swastika! Sparks of excitement shot through his body.

He chuckled. To the housekeeper waiting at the shed doorway he said, "I've found it! It's in bad shape, but I think I can salvage some artifacts to show my students if I may borrow it."

"That's what Mrs. Berkeley said to do, so I guess it's okay. I've written up a receipt for one canvas bag if you'd like to sign it."

"Of course I will. I wonder if you have another large bag, maybe two, that I can slide it into. I'm afraid it will fall apart if I try to pick it up unsupported."

He lifted the fragile treasure into doubled shopping bags and put it in the trunk of his car, hoping he wasn't releasing any tenants.

Later at Susan's, Tom said, "It's not the most glitzy treasure I've seen, but it looks like a gold strike to me. Great work, Max. I'll bring it to Boston this afternoon. My guys at the office are amazing at putting pieces of evidence back together. It may take a while, so please keep Paul with you while we work on this. Meanwhile, I'll call my foreman right now and quit my job. How about a celebration dinner. Pick Paul up. I'm buying."

They went to the Roundup, making sure they ordered something with bones for Shasta.

A middle-aged woman sitting at the table across the aisle said to her husband, "Look at those friends across the way, Teddy, thoroughly enjoying each other's company, laughing and telling stories. The skinny one just recited a limerick that made them all roar with laughter. Wouldn't it be wonderful to be so young and carefree?"

18

Henry Plays His Ace

At the August 23rd meeting of the Oakhill School Board the chairman introduced me to the board as its newest member. "Thank you for allowing me to finish out the two years left on Mr. Blake's term. I'm looking forward to working with you and I have some ideas about putting a different spin on the image of the board."

"We're happy to have you aboard, Mr. Miller," the chairman said, "and if you have anything for us to ponder, we'd be happy to hear it. A new perspective always brings a fresh approach to the work." He knew exactly what I had in mind. At our meeting the week before I told him I didn't want to step on anyone's toes, but I had information I believed should be spoken aloud.

"Thank you, Mr. Chairman. There are two things I have in mind. First, it seems to me we're two organizational levels away from our clients, the students. And the image of the board is a rather stodgy one. Our difficult work is not very glamorous. So, I'd like to propose that we kick off the school year with a contest for junior and senior students, and a scholarship for incentive.

"Now, I believe if I asked everyone in this room to name their favorite high school teacher, you could. Everyone has someone who made a lasting impression on them. I'd like to suggest an essay contest called 'My Favorite Teacher at Oakhill High.' It should be only juniors and seniors so contestants will have the opportunity to experience a wide range of teachers before entering. The five most expressive essays could be read at an assembly. Public speaking is as important in life as writing. The winner could be honored at graduation with the presentation of the scholarship. So, for the whole year the School Board would be involved with students, and we would discover who among our teachers is doing exceptional work ... often not an easy thing to determine."

"I see you have thought this program through carefully, Mr. Miller. What say the Board? Shall we appoint Mr. Miller in charge of the Oakhill School Board Annual Essay Contest? All in favor."

Unanimous "Aye" from the body.

"Thank you for your vote," I said. "I'll start on it right away for the new school year.

"Now for the second point. It's not as positive, I'm afraid. You may know that we at the *Chronicle* invite five students each summer to work as interns at the paper. I started the program at *City News* years ago and several students discovered a passion for journalism they wouldn't have known otherwise.

"For three weeks interns work in every aspect of the newspaper business. They go to Red Sox games with the sports reporter, they shadow reporters on crime and fire scenes, and they follow reviewers of arts and entertainment events. We get to know these students very well. They tell us everything, particularly about their school experience. Well, something they told us about a teacher at the high school concerns me. He's behaving in an erratic fashion."

I paused, allowing the members who were dozing off time to raise their heads and eyebrows at those words.

"A teacher they call Mr. Ski has been using his classroom for a kind of performance center rather than for the important work of teaching American History. The students say it's a 'kick' to be in his class. He allows them to put on musical concerts, to build model toys, to write and perform plays, which it seems to me should be in the English Department, and one thing in particular distresses me."

I had the rapt attention of every board member.

"He, himself, comes to class in costume. In fact, he has been known to be in his class dressed ... in women's clothing."

Pause, letting that one sink in.

"I'll never understand his reasoning, but he allowed one of his students to photograph him, with a group of other students, in his wig and female clothing. I have a copy because the photographer happened to be one of the interns at the paper last summer. The photo is signed 'Eleanor, on the occasion of visiting Mr. Ski's American History class', and it's dated March 18th, 1960."

He passed the photo around for all to enjoy.

"Now, the history of America is a serious subject, not to be taken lightly, or neglected because the teacher is a frustrated performer. Every one of our student interns, and they're at the top of their class, talked and laughed about the antics in Mr. Ski's classroom. This is a conservative town. I don't think the citizens who elected us would stand for this kind of tomfoolery if they were aware of it. I regret having to take this action, but I suggest Mr. Pietrowski be suspended until a thorough investigation can be made of these activities. Thank you for your attention."

"Has anyone firsthand knowledge of what Mr. Miller has just told us?" the chairman asked. No hands raised. "Then what's the pleasure of the board?" he asked.

"This is disturbing," a women said. "I'm upset just hearing about it."

"I think we'd better do our job and look into the way Mr. Pietrowski has been conducting his classroom," said one of the men.

"Our policy states that the best method of instruction is setting a good example in a staff member's dress and manner. It seems he explicitly defied that mandate," offered another member.

"I'm glad this came to our attention before school starts," said another.

"Would anyone like to make a motion on this matter?" the chair asked.

"I move that Mr. Pietrowski be suspended with pay until we can determine if the manner in which he conducts his classroom is consistent with the policies of integrity and ethics of the Oakhill School Board," said the youngest member.

"Any discussion?" asked the chair.

"Well, that seems fair," said the woman who was disturbed. "We just don't know for sure what's going on here. I guess it's his integrity we're questioning.

"I expect it was difficult for Mr. Miller to present us with this news. Thank you for bringing it to light, Mr. Miller. I'm sure you wouldn't have broached the subject if you weren't thoroughly convinced of its veracity, having heard it directly from students. And there's the evidence of the photograph."

"We definitely should keep him out of the classroom," the man who spoke earlier said. "We wouldn't want parents to get wind of his antics. But I disagree on the issue of pay. I think we should pull his pay. This photo is concrete evidence that he's been neglecting his job. I move to amend the motion to 'suspension without pay.'"

"All in favor of the amendment?" "Aye." "Opposed?" Silence.

"Any other discussion on the amended motion?" Silence. "Then let's take a vote. Madam Secretary would you read the motion please."

"Miss Crowley made the motion, amended by Mr. Stevens, that Mr. Pietrowski be suspended without pay until the Oakhill School Board determines if the manner in which he conducts his classroom is consistent with the board's policies of integrity and ethics."

"All those in favor." "Aye" "Those opposed." Silence. "The motion passes unanimously."

"Madam Secretary, will you please advise the Superintendent's Office to write a letter to Mr. Pietrowski informing him of our action. Suspension will begin at once. Any other business? If not I'll hear a motion to adjourn."

"So move."

"Thank you all, and thank you, Mr. Miller for your courage in bringing this matter to our attention. We look forward to the essay contest. Please call on any board members to help with it. The meeting is adjourned."

Walking down the corridor toward the door, Henry couldn't control the grin spreading across his face. Step number one in the total destruction of the King successfully accomplished by The Black Knight. Next, the Sentry. How can I get a nice piece of flavored meat to that mutt the poet keeps at his house?

The reporter covering school board news rushed past him and out the door, probably grateful to finally have something to write about!

19

Watershed Moment

Reading the letter from the Superintendent's Office hit me like catching a blow to the gut from Floyd Patterson. My legs wobbled. I had to sit down. I read the letter three, four times. I don't believe it! Suspended! I'm a good teacher. I challenge anyone to disprove that.

Miller? But how? What could he have said to the board? I'm finished!

I crumpled the letter into a tight ball and threw it across the room. *Gotta calm myself.* I went to the sink and poured a glass of water, then sipped it slowly. I will not allow that devil to make me have an attack. I could hear Paul working at the typewriter in the office upstairs. I'm glad he's busy. *Breathe. Calm down, Max.*

I snatched the wall phone. "Hi. Susan, I need to talk to you. Can you come over?"

"Be right there, Max. Hold on."

The tone of my voice must have told her something serious had happened. I was still sitting at the kitchen table when she arrived. I couldn't speak, just pointed to the wasted letter. She smoothed it out and read: "Office of the Superintendent ... Mr. Pietrowski, I am writing to inform you ... School Board ... unanimously to suspend your privileges. ... Integrity and ethics ... effective immediately.

"Oh, no. Max. You know who's behind this."

"I'm finished," I said. "I quit dancing around with him. I have nothing to lose now. He's ruined my health for years, and probably my brother's. My marriage is over, and now he's destroyed my teaching career. That's who I am, Sue. I'm going to kill him. Before school starts."

"Max! Don't even think that. Tom has the evidence you found proving he's a German saboteur. It'll just take a few weeks to put him out of our lives forever. Please be patient, Max. You could never kill anyone."

"Watch me."

"Okay ... I will. I'm not leaving your side. If you kill him, I'm your accomplice. I'll be as guilty as you are. So, what's our plan?"

"Don't be ridiculous Susan. I shouldn't have called you. Go home. Get away from me. I'm poison. And I'm a fool. I actually thought I could get my life back. Not worth it now."

"Not a chance. We were together at the beginning, and we'll be together at the end, whatever it is. I'm serious, Max. I'm here to stay."

"Okay. I have his knife. I'm the strong one now. He has political power, but he's physically weak. It'll be easy because I don't care if I'm caught. Nothing left to save. Do you know what happens when a teacher's ethics and integrity are questioned? Even if he exonerates himself, the stain of the accusation is always there. There'll be no more jobs of any kind with children. Friends will shun him because there's always the doubt that there may have been some truth to the story. And the story grows worse with every telling.

"Can you imagine the impact that kind of rejection has on a person? It eats away at his dignity and any hope he may have for a future. My life is over, Sue. I might as well take him with me."

"I agree, you have the strength to crush him physically. But, what if you could crush him intellectually, at his own game? What if you could kill the person he is without ruining your life to do it? If you insist on killing him with his knife, I'm in. But I think it would be more satisfying to watch him destroy himself knowing we set up the circumstances."

"I'm not smart enough to beat him at the game he was trained to do."

"Don't count me out," she said. "Maybe our two minds together are better than his. Listen, if we try something and it doesn't work, you always have the knife. We'll be like the passengers on the *Orient Express*, so we'll each be equally as guilty. Let's think this through. I'd love to watch him squirm, not only for the boxes, but also for the things he's done to Paul. Your decision. I'm with you either way."

"Well ... he'd be terrified if he found out we have his duffle bag. Wish I'd looked more closely at what was in it."

"You saw the uniform. What else?" Susan asked.

"The papers were all chewed up, not much use there. Otherwise I saw a pistol, and the medal with a swastika pinned to the uniform jacket. That's when I knew I had the real thing. Wish I'd kept it for a while to explore the contents. I wonder if Tom will tell us what's in it."

"Let's find out." She handed me the phone.

"Hey, Max. Good to hear from you." Tom said. "I should tell you. George Davis didn't find anything at the hardware stores. Miller must have gotten the ingredients by mail order. We don't need that now, anyway."

"How's the work going on the bag?"

"Slowly. They're piecing together some of the paperwork. Johann Schmidt's testimony verifies that Miller was a saboteur, but we need something with Miller's name or image in the duffle bag to link him to the factory. Otherwise all we have is an interesting World War Two artifact. Don't despair. Our guys are good, and there are more documents to work with."

"Tom, how does a person get to be an agent for the Bureau, like George Davis?"

"Not possible, Max. You're involved with the case. You'd never pass muster even if your record is lily-white. We do have civilian sources, and sometimes we use people who are experts in their field. Because you're a teacher it seemed plausible for you to get the bag as a private citizen, and I'm grateful, but the rest is up to us. Sorry, pal, but you'll have to wait for the trial to participate."

"Worth a shot. Thanks, Tom. Bye."

To Susan, he said, "Struck out. So the uniform and pistol, probably a Luger, are the only things we know for sure are in the bag. We can assume there were explosive devices, but who knows what they might be?"

"Max, did you ever get back to Mrs. Berkeley about finding the bag?"

"No, I didn't, and I promised I would. Her housekeeper must have told her. I signed a receipt, but I did say I'd keep in touch."

"Remember she said her husband collected war memorabilia? I wonder if she'd like to be involved in a sabotage case."

"You mean we should tell her?"

"Well, she's not going to get her bag back. Maybe we should tell her why. Wouldn't it be something if there were a German uniform in her husband's collection? Or a Luger? She loaned us the bag, and she did say her interest was piqued. She's a smart lady, Max. I think it might be a good idea to tell her our secret."

I tipped my head back, closed my eyes, and took a long moment. I looked at Susan, took her hands in mine, and said, "Look at what you've done. You've given me hope. That's a dangerous thing. It can be crushed so easily."

"It's all we have right now. I see tears in your eyes, Max. Go ahead and cry. You deserve it. But hold onto me while you do."

She cradled my head against her shoulder, I quietly let my tears roll down my cheeks, and felt cleansed.

"Better?" she asked

"Yeah, much. Excuse me ... I have to call a lady.

"I'd appreciate it if you'll give Mrs. Berkeley the message that I called. Thank you," I said. "Done. I'll thank her and tell her where the bag is at first, and then I'll see how interested she might be to know more."

"What else besides the bag would shake him up?"

"Well, Tom did mention the name of his companion, Johann Schmidt. If he's still alive he must be in prison. He'd be Miller's age, about forty. Tom said he was taken to the Boston Bureau office to be questioned."

"What if he's in prison in Massachusetts? How could we find that out?"

"He'd be in a Federal Prison, and the only one in Massachusetts is at Fort Devens in Ayer. What if a lady newspaper reporter wanted to interview him about the Brandenburg Commandoes," I said.

"Or if a local history teacher wanted to for his students," Susan added.

"Or both!" we said in unison.

The phone rang.

"Hello, Mrs. Berkeley. I wanted to thank you for letting me borrow the bag. I must tell you it's become evidence in an FBI investigation. I hope it will be returned to you when the case is over, but that may not be for quite a while."

"Really. That's very interesting, Max. What sort of case?"

"Well, it's a long story. Started during the war. I'd like to tell it to you, and I think you would be interested because it involves local people and a property you're familiar with, but—"

"I have an idea," she interrupted. "Why not come down here to Dennis for a visit? It's perfect beach weather. We can chat in comfort, and you can tell me everything. Today is Friday. How about coming this evening for the weekend? Are you free?"

"I am, but I have my brother Paul staying with me, and there's another friend who's involved in the case as well. And then there's Shasta, Paul's dog. They're inseparable."

"Oh, this is a large empty house. Some of my family were down for the week, but they've left, and now the house seems even emptier. I'd love to have all three of you as my guests, as well as Shasta. Throw some bathing suits into the car. Dinner's at six. I'm at 752 Ocean Drive. See you then?"

"Yes, indeed. Thank you very much.

"We've just been invited to the Cape for the weekend. She's interested. Wait until she hears it was Miller who blew up her building. Susan, do you think it's okay to tell her everything?"

"Why not? We can ask for her confidentiality, and I'm sure she'll agree. She's seen a lot more of this world than we have. I haven't met her, but I know I'd trust her. Tell Paul. I'm going home to pack, and I need to make a phone call. When shall I pick you up?"

"I'll pick you up at 2:30," I said. She started to protest. "No, don't say a word, just be ready."

"Whatever you say."

I know what she's thinking right now. We can't get to the Cape without crossing the Canal on either the Bourne or Sagamore Bridge. She's probably expecting I'll ask her to drive when we get close. She's in for a surprise.

···❖···

"I'm glad we left a little early. This Friday afternoon traffic is bad enough, but it will get even worse later," I drove the Bel Air with the top down. In the back seat with Paul, Shasta tipped her nose up into the air to catch the breezes.

"Who are we visiting?" Paul asked.

"Mrs. Berkeley," Susan said. "She's the lady whose family owned the *Chronicle* before *City News* bought it."

"I like the beach. I'm inspired to write every time I'm at the ocean. This will be Shasta's first time. But I probably won't be able to take her on the beach because it's before Labor Day."

"I think Mrs. Berkeley may have her own private little stretch of ocean. Wouldn't worry," Susan said.

I pulled over about two-thirds of the way down to the Cape.

"My turn to drive?" Susan asked.

"No thanks. If no one minds I'd like to put the top up so we can listen to the radio."

"Not at all. Sure," they said.

When we approached the Sagamore Bridge, I caught Susan looking over at me. I concentrated on the road. This is a very high bridge. Huge ships pass underneath it in the Cape Cod Canal. I entered the approach to the bridge in the left hand lane, stayed there, held my breath, and crossed it. Just like that.

The day seemed even more bright and sunny. I proceeded onto Route 6A, past rows of stunted pines toward Dennis, as if this weren't a milestone. Susan leaned over and planted a kiss on my cheek. We both knew why. Paul looked a bit curious, but he was too polite to ask.

20

Cape Cod Magic

The Berkeley house was a cedar shingled Victorian cottage with porches and gables on its own bluff overlooking the ocean. It looked so comfortable and lived-in Susan couldn't wait to get inside. Paul took Shasta for a walk into the trees at the side of the house while Max and Susan unloaded their luggage. They were met by an elderly man who introduced himself as Sidney. He took some of their bags and led them into the house. Mrs. Berkeley greeted them in the foyer.

"Welcome! I'm so happy you could visit. Come in. Cooler in here. The porches keep the house cool, and there's always a breeze off the water. Sidney will bring your things up to your rooms. I've put you and Paul into the same room, Max. I hope that will be fine."

"It is. Thank you for inviting us. Even though we've never actually met I feel as if I know you already."

"And I you."

"This is my friend Susan, and Paul will be along with Shasta. She can stay outside if you'd rather."

"Gracious no, we've always had dogs. German shepherds, in fact. Not for a while now, but this house has seen its share of pooches. Let's have some lemonade, and relax. How was the drive? Fridays can be brutal coming down here."

"It was quite a pleasant drive," Susan said, still elated over Max crossing that bridge.

An elderly woman introduced as Sally served the lemonade.

"I'm fascinated to hear the story of the bag. You said it started during the war?" Mrs. Berkeley asked.

"It did," Max answered. "I should tell you, Paul has a memory problem. I may stop telling the story if I think it will be too much for him to hear."

"Oh that's fine, thank you for the warning," Mrs. Berkeley said.

"In August, 1943," Max said, "we three children were playing in the storage room of the factory."

"At 652 Main Street?" Mrs. Berkeley asked.

"Yes, I thought that might arouse your interest."

Max proceeded to tell her the story of the incident at the boxes, showing her the scar under his chin. "Everyone believed the fire had been caused by lightning, and we were three frightened children who never challenged that story. In fact, I swore everyone to secrecy."

Paul entered the room at that moment with Shasta in tow. "Hello, Mrs. Berkeley. Thank you so much for inviting us. I'm Paul, Max's brother."

"Welcome, Paul. I know who you are. I've read your book, *Echoes*. It's so imaginative and colorful. I thoroughly enjoyed it. And welcome Shasta. You're a beauty. Would you like some lemonade, Paul?"

"Yes, thank you. I took Shasta down to the beach. She started to go into the water, but when the wave receded and made the tinkling noise it does over the pebbles, she backed off as if it was an animal. She's the bravest creature I know, but the new noise startled her. Maybe she'll go in tomorrow."

Sally appeared as if on cue to announce dinner.

A serenity enveloped Susan as she walked into the dining room. She stepped into a painting with a palette of subtle textures and warm hues, waiting for its subjects to arrive for a memory-making dinner. She imagined the cheerful conversations of family seated in the Chippendale chairs surrounding the mahogany table. Blue hydrangea blossoms floated in a cut glass bowl at its center, guarded by two white candles in silver holders, all on a lace cloth.

Children had played here. An assortment of Matchbox cars was parked among the claw feet of the double pedestal table. On the rich red and blue patterned Oriental rug they waited for their drivers to return. How freeing to realize that no one cared if children made a little mess. Susan pictured a Christmas dinner with logs burning in the tile-surrounded fireplace, keeping the family cozy and warm. *How I'd love to have a family of my own gather in a room like this one day.*

The only electric lights in the room were two sconces flanking the mirror above the fireplace, but candles had been lit on both the large and smaller tables. Six-foot tall windows were dressed with sheers that floated, wave-like, with each breeze, and a door at the far end of the room led to the side porch. Ivory grasscloth, the color of old piano keys, covered the walls. "This room is lovely," Susan said.

"Thank you, Susan. Yes, it's my favorite room in the house. We've had many family gatherings here. It's comfortable all year 'round. We're sitting at the children's table. More cozy."

After a sumptuous dinner of roasted chicken and summer vegetables, they enjoyed apple pie and ice cream for dessert. Then Paul took Shasta to the kitchen to feed her and take her for a walk.

"You know, we bought the factory building in '45," Mrs. Berkeley said. "The renovation took over a year but we considered it well worth the effort to restore it. The building has amazing architectural detail, and the exterior wasn't damaged by the fire.

"So, the bag under the stairs belonged to a German saboteur. And none of you has ever told the story of this Heinrich Mueller?"

"Not until we met FBI Agent Tom Hanson," Max said. "We proved, to ourselves, and to the FBI, that Heinrich Mueller is Henry Miller, the person from *City News* who is Managing Editor of the *Chronicle*."

Mrs. Berkeley winced at his words. "Horrible thought."

"Paul doesn't remember any of it. That may be merciful. But anyone knowing the facts of that day, and reading *Echoes*, would think he does." Then Max told Mrs. Berkeley about the crimes against Paul, and about his own terrible news earlier today.

"I had learned about the board's action before I talked to you today, Max," Mrs. Berkeley said. "It's in the *Chronicle*. It shocked me to read it. I'm pleased you called. Hearing what you've been through, I will do whatever I can to help resolve this nightmare. My husband and I are being violated as well since that person is in our building, running our paper."

"Thank you," Max said. "I'm not sure what any of us can do, but I recall you said your husband collected war memorabilia. The only things I saw in the duffle bag were a German Army uniform and a Luger pistol. If either of those things is in his collection perhaps we might borrow them and try to make Miller show his hand. So far as the community is concerned he's clear of any wrongdoing. Oakhill sees him as a model citizen. I worry he may do more damage before we can detain him.

"Tom says the FBI will eventually have enough evidence to bring him to trial, but that process may take weeks. This has gone on long enough. I worry about what he'll do to Paul next, and he knows who Susan is now. I need to protect the people I love. If we can fluster him enough to make a careless move, maybe we can make the case proceed more quickly."

"Let's sleep on it and see what our brains come up with. You do realize your friend Tom would not approve of your taking any action at all," Mrs. Berkeley said.

"I do, and he's been terrific," Max said, "but I offered to work on the case and apparently that's not appropriate. This is my fight, it's personal."

For the rest of the evening the four friends joined in animated conversation, much of it concerning the time Mr. and Mrs. Berkeley ran the *Chronicle*. Shasta lay by Paul's feet the whole time, picking up her head only when she heard her name.

As they started up the stairs Mrs. Berkeley said, "Breakfast at 8:30. Sleep well."

A four-poster bed with white embroidered pillowcases and a puffy white down comforter took center stage of Susan's room. A lady's chair with a back-splat carved in a grape pattern sat by the window, and an antique wardrobe dominated the wall across from the bed. Susan opened the wardrobe door and discovered her clothes had been carefully hung inside.

Finding her pajamas in a drawer of the tiny white milk-painted chest, she started to get ready for bed. This has been the most unusual day of my life. It began with my agreeing to be complicit in murder, I got to comfort my friend as he wept, and it ended at the loveliest beach house I've ever seen. Did Max really say, "the people I love"? Well, there are all kinds of love, and we are each other's best friends again.

If I'm honest, I'd say we fell in love when we were kids, maybe the day he took my mom and me to Grant's for my first pair of dungarees. He held my hand walking across Main Street when the light turned red and yellow. No one made jeans for girls then, but we found the perfect boy's dungarees for me. He convinced my mother to buy them. He said,

"Now you'll be able to keep up with me in the hills out back."

She took the silver clips out of her hair and began brushing. He was adventurous, and creative ... a risk taker, and a caring friend. Seems like his reactions to the violence squeezed all the spirit out of him, except maybe in his classroom. Now he's made a choice to change his life, and he's acting on it. When I see him getting stronger I'm reminded of the boy he was, and I envision the person he's becoming. And I'm flooded with, what? Warmth? Pride? I don't know. It's just such a beautiful thing to see.

She walked down the corridor to the massive bathroom with both a clawfoot tub and modern shower. She washed her face and brushed her teeth, then returned to nestle under the down comforter. Closing her eyes she let the sound of the pounding surf lull her to sleep.

Max lay in his bed, wide awake. What a dilemma. There are pieces of hard evidence. Why can't I come up with a way to use them, to stop him now, before he does something else? I have to protect Susan.

He let his mind drift to Susan. I said, "the people I love" about Paul and Susan. It's so natural. I do love her. Truth to tell, I think I've loved her since we were kids. But trying to contain my terrors changed me. No more. I need to become my genuine self, whatever that is. Then I'll be worthy of telling her how I feel. The time will come. Gotta watch out for Michael Hathaway.

He seems determined to come back into her life. She says it's a friendship. I worry I could lose her if I don't act soon.

She loves me too. She doesn't know it yet, but she does. She held me in the darkest moment of my life. And that kiss on the cheek to celebrate the bridge. She loves the real me, a healthy me. Honestly caring about the happiness and wellbeing of another person, that's real love. Unfortunately it might make a person behave irrationally. She did offer to commit murder for me. True love may be the most powerful force on the planet.

"Yes," he said, bolting upright. He checked to be sure he hadn't wakened Paul, or worse, Shasta. Then he relaxed, and let himself be carried by the sounds of the surf into welcomed sleep.

Saturday started out as one of those gorgeous days that can happen only on Cape Cod. "The sun shines differently down here," Susan said at breakfast. "It's warmer, enticing everyone to go outside and play."

"And that is what we'll do today," Mrs. Berkeley said.

They played several spirited games of croquet on the side lawn. Max, Paul and Susan went for a refreshing swim while Mrs. Berkeley and Shasta watched from under an umbrella on the beach. Shasta continued to avoid the strange sounds made by the receding waves, but she napped while Mrs. Berkeley read her book. After lunch, Paul took Shasta for a walk, saying he might do some writing.

"You both look well rested," Mrs. Berkeley said to Max and Susan. "So much more relaxed than when you arrived. This place has a way of helping people do that, and to think more clearly."

"It does," Max said. "I had the best night's sleep I've had in ages."

"Me too," Susan said. "Coming down here has turned out to be the best medicine for both of us."

"Well, let's let the Cape magic keep working," Mrs Berkeley said. "No serious discussions today, but we'll get back to the subject when we've all let our minds work on it a bit longer. Now, how about a nice walk around the neighborhood?"

Paul returned just before five, with sheaves of paper and a big grin.

"This is the most inspiring place. Max, did I spend time at the ocean before I can remember?"

"No, we took a few day trips to the shore at Davenport, but nothing significant. We all were fish at one time in our evolution though, so maybe it's the echo of that time making you want to write. I'm glad, whatever it is."

After dinner Mrs. Berkeley grinned and said, "Come with me," leading them down some stairs to a small projection room. "Harold and I had this room built when the grandchildren visited for a week at a time. The Cape is grand in the sunshine, but a rainy day with three young children can be challenging. My friends in California send me copies of old movies, especially ones about newspaper reporters. There's a stack of them. Choose one."

"Mrs. Berkeley, this is exactly what we did as children. Every Saturday we went to the movies, then we'd play in the boxes at being those characters. We love movies," Max said.

They chose *Meet John Doe*, with Gary Cooper and Barbara Stanwyk. Max set up the projector and they watched the film about the power of the press to generate a national social movement.

After breakfast the next morning Max told Susan and Mrs. Berkeley the plan he had devised.

"I like it," Mrs. Berkeley said. "I believe in the premise, and I think it will be effective. I have a plan of my own. I've decided that no matter what you do, I will address the Oakhill School Board. I believe I still have some clout in that town.

"I've thought about the sale of the *Chronicle*. There's nothing legally I can do about Miller's job at the paper, but addressing the school board is something I can do. And I need to do it, just as much as you need to protect Susan and Paul. I can't just stand by and let years of Howard's and my work be defiled by that person managing our paper."

As they were leaving Max said, "Thank you so much for everything, Mrs. Berkeley. For the wonderful weekend, and for your confidence in me."

"My pleasure, my boy. You must visit again. Please keep me advised as to your plans, so I can make mine."

"Absolutely."

"Thank you," Paul said. "I left a poem for you on the children's table. I had a great time."

She hugged Susan, saying, "It's such a pleasure to see two people so much in love. Old memories. Please take care of yourself, and keep in touch."

"I will. Thank you," Susan said, a bit surprised at Mrs. Berkeley's words.

On the way home Max told Susan, "We'll go back to Oakhill first and see if Maria can stay at my house for a few days. Then we'll take the business trip we talked about, okay?"

"That's a deal."

21

You Always Meet Twice

When Max and Susan were on the road again, he said, "I should tell you, driving over the bridge to the Cape wasn't a miracle like something out of a Dickens novel." He guided the Bel Air south, toward the Mass. Pike. "I've been working on my immunity program for about three weeks, trying to get myself in balance. I'd driven over a few bridges before I got to the Sagamore, but that was the highest of them all."

"About three weeks," Susan said. "That's since you've been on your own, then."

"Yeah. It's my battle, but your encouragement did inspire me. Some of it's been a struggle, but no attacks. I feel like I'm over the hump. After conquering whatever goal I set for myself, even the small ones, I feel euphoric. I really wanted to tell you, but I wanted to show you more. I'd planned to drive to the Cape as my Performing Knowledge presentation, and I did."

"Max, I believe you're becoming the person you were always intended to be. You amaze me, Mr. Ski."

"I only hope my kids can call me that again. First we have a few bridges to cross in Connecticut today."

At the hotel in Beechwood, New York, Max looked up the phone numbers and addresses for Henry and Lila Miller, and for Trudy Mueller. "Let's visit Mom first. Twenty-six Bond Street." He called Trudy at about six on Sunday evening. "We're acquaintances of Henry's from the war days. We'd like to come by to visit if you're free. We have some belongings of his I'd like to show you."

"Of course, come ahead. I've just finished having dinner. You can join me in a glass of iced tea."

"Welcome," Trudy said with a smile as she opened the door. "I always enjoy meeting friends of Heinrich's. I still can't get used to calling him Henry." She led them into the living room. "Please sit down. You said you knew him when he was in the service?"

"Yes," Max said. "Some of what we're about to tell you may be hard to hear, Mrs. Mueller, but every word is true."

"Of course." She wondered if he might tell her how Heinrich had been wounded.

"We met Heinrich on August 16th, 1943. We were children at the time."

Max told the story of the boxes, objectively and honestly. He showed her the knife, and his scar. Then he recounted the incidents since Miller's return to Oakhill, showing her a copy of *Echoes,* and the three feathers. He explained their significance, and told her where they had been left.

"My brother could have died in the fire if not for his dog's insistence on waking him. Heinrich has attacked Paul twice and me once, and now he knows who Susan is. Mrs. Mueller, I know you love your son, and if you will help us stop him now, another tragedy can be avoided. If you can't, I will stop him before he gets a chance to hurt Susan. The FBI has all the evidence it needs to detain him, but processing it may take enough time for him to strike again."

"You're correct. I do love my son, as does his wife who is the loveliest, most compassionate person you could meet. You have filled in some questions for me, like why he would never tell us where he was stationed in the war, and why he didn't take advantage of the veteran's services when he needed therapy. We only wanted him to be well, to recover from his wounds."

Trudy paused. "I don't want to believe what you have told me about my boy is true. But I can believe some of it. His father died when Heinrich was a teenager, a vulnerable time in a boy's life. Then he came under the influence of the leader of our German Club who, let's be honest, supported Hitler. Otto would not have allowed his son to be influenced by the Nazis, but I regret, I did allow it.

"So, you see, Mr. Pietrowski, I don't believe Heinrich is entirely to blame for his actions. The adults in his life were faithful to our German heritage, and he sensed it. I don't think that's such a bad thing. He might not even have known about Hitler's deeds at the time. If what you say is true, whatever Heinrich did during the war was his duty as a German soldier.

"And those accusations about your recent problems in Oakhill. Well, I'm certainly not convinced my son is involved in any of that irrational behavior. The person who did those things could be anyone who has read your brother's book and taken the subject to heart, even an avid fan. No, I can't believe my son could behave in that manner.

"So, Mr. Pietrowski, my son may have been a German saboteur during the war, as you contend. I believe he had good reason to want to defend Germany. Otherwise I think you're using him as a scapegoat ... someone to blame your problems on."

"Mrs. Mueller," Max said, "as long as Henry's in America, what he did during the war is criminal. Whether we stop him now or the FBI does later, he will probably be tried as a saboteur. Then he'll be stripped of his American citizenship, serve prison time, and be sent back to Germany. When I called to visit his companion, Johann Schmidt, at the Fort Devens prison they told me he had been released and no longer lives in the United States."

"I remember Johann," Trudy said. "Shy boy, but very bright. He grew up here in Beechwood. He visited Berlin in '38 with Heinrich. His parents moved away several years ago. I wonder if they went back to Germany with him."

"I can't imagine how difficult it must be for you to hear all this," Max said. "We understand if you choose not to be involved."

"If the FBI contacts me I'll know it's because of my son's allegiance during the war. But I do not believe your outlandish accusations about the events in Oakhill. Good day to you both."

In the car Susan broke the silence. "What now, Mr. Ski?"

"It's only seven thirty. Let's call on Mrs. Miller."

They pulled up to the low-slung ranch style house surrounded by shade trees. Lila answered the doorbell. "Mrs. Miller. I apologize for not calling. I'm Max Pietrowski. My friend Susan and I know Henry from years ago. We're traveling through the state and thought we'd stop by to say hello."

"What a pleasant surprise. I'm sorry, but Henry isn't here right now. But do come in. We can chat and I'll tell him you were here."

As they walked through the living room onto a screened porch Max noticed a teen-age boy working with pencil and paper at the kitchen table. "Let's sit out here so Jeffrey won't be disturbed. He's taking French this summer to help with his college applications. So, when did you meet Henry?"

"His name was Heinrich at the time." Max related the story exactly as he had told it to Trudy.

"That's quite a tale, Mr. Pietrowski. Do you have any proof of what you've told me?"

"We do Mrs. Miller," Susan said. "We have his German companion Johann's testimony naming Heinrich as a saboteur, and we found a bag with a German uniform and medal which were at the factory. But, more importantly, I remember him."

"But you were children."

"Some events one never forgets." Susan crossed her arms to ward off a chill. "I expect you remember things when you were nine as well. I recall every second of that day."

"And the more recent events in Oakhill. How can you be certain it's not some unhappy person looking for attention from your brother?"

"Too much of a coincidence," Max said. "Henry shows up back in Oakhill and two of the three people who thwarted his mission are targeted? In the *Chronicle's* announcement of his new job there I read that he had been the arts reporter at *City News*. He's read *Echoes*, Mrs. Miller. We hope you see the urgency of ending Henry's destructive behavior now, before anything worse happens."

Lila sat silently a long moment. She sighed and closed her eyes. "My husband is amazing. He's the most courageous person I know. He deals with pain from his injuries every day. He not only copes, he endures." She looked up at Max. "However, I am aware of some behaviors that he doesn't know I've witnessed. I need some time to process what you have told me. Can you come back tomorrow afternoon, around three?"

"Of course," Max said.

Back at the hotel Max led Susan into the restaurant. "I'm starving."

"No wonder. It's nearly nine thirty."

A quick look at the menu and they ordered two steak dinners. "It's in their hands now." Max folded his hands and leaned back. "The two people in the world Miller loves most. Let's not think about the outcome until we see Lila tomorrow. This looks delicious."

"Let's have coffee upstairs," Susan said after a shared chocolate mousse. "I want to kick my shoes off."

They went into their adjoining rooms and Max knocked on Susan's door. "Come in, Max." She stood barefoot at the kitchenette, ripped open the first coffee packet, and poured the contents into a plastic cup.

Max followed her to the counter.

"Here to help?"

"Turn around," he said.

She did, holding the packet filed with the next aromatic measure of coffee. He took it from her hand and put it on the counter. He planned to kiss her for the first time, and he wanted her fully in this moment with him. Putting his hands on her waist, he drew her toward him. He bowed his head toward hers and brushed her lips, warm and full, with his. He caught a faint scent of wild rose, her cologne.

She hesitated.

Then she lifted her lips to his, inviting him. Her arms went to his shoulders, and the back of his neck. He clutched her in his arms, no longer able to contain the desire he'd caged for so long. He kissed her from the depths of his being. The energy between them intensified as her body responded to him.

He released her and slid his hand into her hair. He held her head close to him, kissing her forehead. He wanted her to know she'd always be safe in his arms. Her heart hammered against his chest.

He lifted her chin to look into her face. "I love you, Susan. I've been aching to say that for so long. We belong together." He raised his eyebrows. "How would you like to play Guard the Castle ... for the rest of our lives?"

"I might indeed, my wise and noble king, but I can't ... I'm engaged."

The words slapped Max across the face. "What? Is it Michael?"

"He's been asking me for a while. Last week I accepted."

"Do you love him?"

Susan didn't answer. Then she said, "I love that he loves me, and I love being married. It seemed like the rational thing to do. But I don't feel with him like I do right now."

"Sue, I'm drowning here."

"Then we'll rescue each other just in the nick o' time. I told myself the warmth I felt was pride when I watched you tackling your fears, and friendship when I heard you say, 'the people I love.' But this is what love feels like ... you're the man I love, Max."

He enfolded her in his arms again with a huge sigh, weak in the knees with relief. He kissed her forehead. "That night at the Cape I felt the strength of my feelings for you. I knew two things. I'd risk my life for you, and love is the most powerful force on the planet. So powerful that even a hardened criminal may be shattered if he knew how much he'd hurt the people he cares for."

"And Miller went home to his mom's house when he was injured. That boy has a special place in his heart for his mother."

"Exactly."

"Do you want to know what I think is the best part of this whole ordeal?" Susan grinned up at Max.

"Yes, you and I."

"Okay, then, second best."

"No, what?"

"Well, however it ends, it's such a good story that I may be inspired to find a book in it."

"I know you will. And they'll be others too. We've uncovered our demons, Sue. We shined a light on the twisted beliefs from our past that were holding us back. We met each one head on."

"... and exposed the lies in the lessons they were trying to teach us."

"Right. You said it earlier. We found our path to becoming the people we were always intended to be. It may be a lifelong journey, but at least we know the way." He held her body close. "I'm so grateful I found you again. I can't wait to discover the rest of my life with you."

The next afternoon Susan and Max found Trudy waiting for them at Lila's house. "Lila shared some information with me that has influenced my decision regarding my son. Apparently he's more troubled by his injuries than I had known.

"Over the years I've come to believe my friend Dieter who has always maintained my husband was murdered by the Nazis. I have no proof, of course, they're too smart for that. As soon as we arrived here, Otto embraced the American values of free speech and equal opportunity, and expressed his opinions openly. I took longer to be comfortable, but eventually I learned to be grateful for the chance to be an American.

"Because of what I learned today, and because I'm convinced Otto died defending this country, I need to honor his convictions and his memory by setting this dreadful business straight. What shall I do?"

On Wednesday, August 30th at noon, Fred entered Henry Miller's office saying, "There are some people here to see you, Mr. Miller."

"Who are they, Fred?"

"Don't know, but they look like friendly folk."

"Okay, show them in," Henry said. Leaning on his cane he stood to greet his visitors.

Trudy walked in first.

"Mama. What a surprise. So good to see you. Are you on a shopping trip to the Design Center in Boston?" He walked around the desk to give her a hug.

"Hello, Heinrich. No, we're here just to see you, dear. We'd like to have a chat."

As Katrina entered the office, he said, "Trini! This is great. Two of my favorite people in the world." He hugged them both.

Following behind Katrina, Lila said, "Hello Henry."

"Hey, is this my birthday or something? What a nice surprise. Hi Honey." He kissed her on the cheek.

Then Paul and Shasta entered the office. Henry protested. "What are you doing here? Get that mutt out of here. No dogs allowed in this building. I'm busy. Leave my office at once!"

"Hello, Mr. Miller. I'm Paul Pietrowski, and I have some business to take up with you today."

Susan walked in, then Max. He closed the door behind him.

"What's going on? You three are not welcome here. Get out." Henry shouted, "Fred, Fred come in here!"

"Fred will not be coming in, Miller," Max said. "Your mother has something of yours she wants to return to you."

"Heinrich." Trudy met his gaze and clasped his hands in hers. "We know these people. We know everything, dear. There are no more secrets between us. We know about Brandenburg, and about the factory fire here in 1943."

Henry stiffened. "Mama! What have they been telling you? Stories with no proof! A pack of lies! Let them prove their lies. I don't know what you've heard, Mama, but I've done nothing wrong. I'm just trying to run this paper, and be a good citizen. Please don't believe any slander against me by these hateful people. Let them prove their claims ... they can't!"

Trudy took an envelope from her purse. With a barely audible sob, she removed the trench knife from it, and put it down on Henry's desk.

Henry looked at the knife, then searched his mother's face. "Mama, where did you get that?" He reached out and touched the handle. "It's my knife. I lost it in the ... Oh, no. Mama, please don't look so sad. I only acted to protect Germany. I was never a Nazi. I was innocent during the war of anything except defending our Fatherland.

"We were Commandos. We always believed Germany was in the right. Fact is, I was trained to dismiss the enemy propaganda about Germany that I heard here. It wasn't until long after the war ended that I understood what Hitler and his Nazis did.

"And the pay was so good. I could help support you and Katrina. I knew Papa would have been proud of me, of what I could do for Germany, and for you."

"I believe those were your intentions, dear," she said, "and they are honorable ones, but you were just a boy when you joined the Commandoes. You were too young at the time to exercise good judgment, and your father wasn't here to guide you. He became a loyal American, Heinrich. I believe he died defending this country, just like any American soldier on a battlefield. If he had lived he'd never have let you become a Commando."

Trudy paused, took a deep breath, then said, "Heinrich, we also know about what's happened since you moved back here to Oakhill ... about the destruction at Paul's house, the fire in the forest, and your presentation to the school board. We know these people are the children in the factory, dear. Lila and I have read *Echoes*."

Then Lila approached the desk. "Henry," she said, "the most important thing we know dear, is we love you, and we forgive you." She removed an envelope from her purse, and let three red-tipped black feathers float out.

Covering his face with his hands, Henry put his head down and slumped into a chair. Trudy drew a chair up to face his. She took both his hands and held them in hers. "Heinrich, dear, your father and I were desperate when we came here. America welcomed us, allowed us to work hard and make a good living. America healed your father's spirit and gave us back our dignity. "He would have put you on the right track, in a different direction, but I didn't have the wisdom to do it. We all have to deal with the consequences of our behavior. It's time for you, and for me, to face up to our actions of today, and of years ago."

Max stepped forward. "Look, Miller, even I can understand your intentions for the incident in '43. But, German soldier or not, you're still responsible for what you did. The lives of a hundred families were torn apart by the devastation you caused here.

"Coming back here to terrorize us is a different story. It's not only criminal, it's ... insane. You need help, Miller."

Henry's body tensed. He sat up straight, his eyes glued to Max's. "You!" he spat out. "You and your bratty little friends. You're to blame for all this." His once silky voice became grating. "That building should have been empty. I should have killed you when I had the chance." He pushed himself out of the chair and lunged at Max, throwing his cane ahead of him.

Trudy shouted, "Heinrich, No!" Lila and Katrina shrieked.

Each split second felt like a minute. Max crouched, waiting for the cane to reach him. He waved it away with his right forearm, and welcomed Henry's charge. Yeah! Come on. Start something I can finish. You don't deserve an easy out. If you wanna throw the first punch, let's go! Max clenched his fist so hard the nails bit into his flesh. At close range he unwound with an uppercut to Millers' chin. Miller flew onto his back. Max rushed towards him, grabbed him by the jacket to throw the next blow, and ... froze. Miller had lost his balance completely. He was limp. All the fight out of him.

"You're not worth my effort, Miller. Now it's your turn to face your demons."

Max picked Henry up under the arms like a child, put an arm around his back, and carried him to the chair. Paul had to restrain Shasta who wanted to get into the fray. Max gestured to Paul, "I'm okay." He walked toward the office door and kicked the cane away, hard. He raked his fingers through his hair. Susan turned toward him and put her hand on his shoulder.

Trudy rushed to Henry. She held and rocked him. "I'm okay, Mama. I'm so sorry. I hate this ... to see you hurt because of what I've done. I did my best for my country. Here I only wanted justice for my injuries. It's who I became at Brandenburg." Henry collapsed, head down on his mother's shoulder, weeping. Through his sobs he said, "I'm trapped. I'll go to prison. I'll be put in a cell for the rest of my life. I'm finished, I'm dead."

Lila bent down to put her arms around his shaking shoulders and said in that serene voice, "Oh no, you are not, Henry. We are going to wipe the slate clean and start again. I will never leave you, but it's time to end this turmoil. Perhaps a compassionate judge will take into account how much you've already suffered. Whatever happens, you're my husband for the rest of my life."

Katrina stood with both hands on her mother's shoulders, showing her support, but too choked up to speak.

Two Oakhill police officers entered the office from the back room. One picked up the knife and feathers from the desk, the other grasped Henry. They escorted him out of the office and through the distribution room to a waiting unmarked car. Lila took Max's hand as she passed him and said a tearful, "Goodbye." They left for the Boston Office of the FBI.

After taking a few calming breaths, Max picked up Miller's phone and called Tom Hanson. "Hi Tom, Max Pietrowski here. Just want to let you know that Henry Miller and his family will be arriving at your office with an Oakhill Police escort in about forty minutes. He's decided to turn himself in ...

"Yes, that's right. They'll tell you everything when they get there. I'm in his office now. Thanks for everything. Susan, Paul and I appreciate all the work you've done to help us. I'll call you tomorrow to fill in our side of the details." He looked up at Susan. "That was a sad scene. The man was destroyed. Are you okay, Sue?"

"Yes, I am."

"Paul, how are you?"

"I'm fine. I'm relieved to know the person pretending to be The Black Knight has been stopped. Thank you, Max. Why did he frighten me so much? He's so weak. I'll take Shasta out to the car."

"I expected to be elated when I saw him crumble," Max said. "I'm not. It was ... pitiful."

"And powerful," Susan said. "He's a lucky man to have his family care that much about him."

"Paul's right," Max said. "We gave him influence over our lives he didn't deserve. I'm glad this plan worked."

"You did it, Max. You took him down your own way. I see my old risk-taking friend back again. And now I recognize the familiar warm feeling that came over me when I saw you being kind to the person who tried to ruin your life. I love you, Max." She stood on tiptoes to kiss him.

"Sweetie, that makes it all worthwhile. Now, I have to call a lady.

"Mrs. Berkeley. Miller has just been taken to the FBI office in Boston. It happened with the help of his family. He's finally out of our lives. Thank you for your help ... Yes, you really did help. You can't imagine how important our visit to the Cape was. It allowed us to take a fresh perspective on the whole matter ... I appreciate whatever you'd like to do. Yes, I'll keep in touch, bye."

···❖···

The Oakhill School Superintendent's Office put out a bulletin stating that an emergency meeting of the School Board had been called for Wednesday, August 30th, seven p.m. at Oakhill High School. Mrs. Howard Berkeley asked to address the board regarding its recent suspension of a staff member. She chastised them for being "hoodwinked" by their newest member, Mr. Henry Miller. She allowed it may be understandable, as Mr. Miller was thoroughly trained in the skill of deception. But a talented teacher, Max Pietrowski, had been victimized.

Mrs. Berkeley insisted on the immediate revocation of the suspension order. She told the board that, "all will be apparent soon, but to prolong the agony of any further delay in keeping this creative, exceptional teacher from his job would be a crime."

She offered to take full responsibility for the actions of Mr. Pietrowski as she knows him to be an, "honest, ethical person of impeccable integrity." The board voted unanimously to rescind their order.

On the way home from Miller's office, Max dropped Paul and Shasta off at the cabin, and continued to Susan's apartment. "Are you okay?" she asked. "I mean the murder's off. Are you disappointed?"

"Not funny. I was serious. I don't want to spend any time thinking about that person again. How about a coffee."

"You got it," she said as they entered her building.

He sat in the old wicker chair. She went into the kitchen, rattled some pots, and turned on the tap. He followed her into the kitchen. "I can't wait for coffee."

She turned toward him. "Oh, you have to leave?"

"No," He enfolded her in his arms. "I have to hold you right now." He drew her close, caught the familiar scent of her wild rose cologne. "And I never did hear your answer. Will you marry me?"

She looked into his eyes and grinned. "Yes! I will, my wise and noble king."

About the Author

Jeanette Scales has been a teacher, private school director, and director of the adult education program in her town. She owned an interior design company in Massachusetts for ten years, and an inn in New Hampshire for twenty. While operating the inn she founded a jewelry design company and started writing her novel, Boxes. Jeanette sold the inn, moved back to Massachusetts, and is looking forward to finishing her second novel. Her website address is **www.jeanettescales.com.**

Made in the USA
Middletown, DE
28 February 2016